Arthur Hugh Urquhart Colquhoun

The Hon. James R. Gowan, C.M.G., Q.C., LL. D.

Member of Canadian Senate : A Memoir

Arthur Hugh Urquhart Colquhoun

The Hon. James R. Gowan, C.M.G., Q.C., LL. D.
Member of Canadian Senate : A Memoir

ISBN/EAN: 9783337170769

Printed in Europe, USA, Canada, Australia, Japan

Cover: Foto ©Raphael Reischuk / pixelio.de

More available books at **www.hansebooks.com**

MEMBER OF CANADIAN SENATE.

A MEMOIR.

EDITED BY

A H. U. COLQUHOUN, B.A.

TORONTO:
1894.

PREFACE.

IN the preparation of this Memoir for the press, invaluable assistance has been rendered by a member of the Bar, born in the district where Senator Gowan lived for fifty years, and where he now resides, and one who, moreover, has known him personally for over thirty years. Forming also a basis for the present work are a number of sketches, already published, covering many incidents in the Senator's career, and numerous cuttings from the public press respecting him. Of all these free use has been made, particularly of a brochure by a "Member of the Bar of Ontario," published in 1890.

These and other trustworthy sources of information have furnished material for a fuller and more complete narrative of the public services and career of Senator Gowan than has, the Editor believes, yet appeared, and it is hoped that the Memoir may satisfy the wishes of friends for some more ample and complete record than anyone now living could supply from his own memory.

The Memoir, however, is not without general interest in connection with early progress in this Province, for few of the pioneers still living have taken a more varied part in the working and development of its institutions— legal, municipal and educational—than Senator Gowan. Though in his seventy-ninth year, the honorable gentleman retains his vigor unimpaired, and years of usefulness may still be before him.

When a complete story of his life is told, with the aid of a mass of correspondence between him and the public men he knew and was connected with in work— correspondence which he is believed to have carefully preserved—when such a work comes to be written it will fill many gaps in the present brief Memoir, and throw urther light on a busy life of conspicuous devotion to public duty and public interests. In the meantime, the honorable gentleman's friends and relatives, with the little volume now presented to them, can form some idea of the work in which he has taken part, and the services he has rendered as a public man.

A. H. U. COLQUHOUN.

TORONTO, *January*, *1894*.

―――――

A BRIEF glance at the early condition of this Province and its after progress, seems a fitting introduction to a compendious biographical notice of a public servant, whose appointment to office occurred over fifty years ago.

Upper Canada, Ontario as it is now called, the premier Province in the great Canadian confederation, first in population, first in wealth and material progress, and conspicuous for the excellence of its legal, municipal, and educational systems, had a grand origin.

At the close of the last century it was largely settled by a body of energetic and patriotic men, who abandoned their properties and home ties in the United States to carve out for themselves new homes in the forest land of Upper Canada, where the flag they and their fathers loved would consecrate a new Britain, and enable them still to glory in the fact that they were part and parcel of the greatest Empire the world has ever known. From the early part of this century, its population has increased by a healthy immigration, year after year, of hardy and enterprising settlers, direct from the British Isles ; and possessing as it did, an immense area of fertile land surrounded by inland seas, affording great facilities for approach and internal communication, and a glorious climate ; the country naturally offered marked inducements to the settler, and the prospects of a grand future. By an Act of the Imperial Parliament in 1791, the Province was given a constitution similar to that of the mother land, enabling the **Legisla-ture** of the country to make laws for the peace, **welfare** and **good government** of the Colony, and to maintain a system **of** government suited to their condition. In **a** word, the inhabitants of Upper **Canada** were enabled **to** solve the problem of maintaining the rights **and** liberties of the people, and **developing material progress** through safe democratic **institutions, under and in connection** with the greatest of European **monarchies.**

Warmly attached to British institutions and laws, the first Act passed in the first session of the first Parliament of Upper Canada, adopted the laws of England, **and de-clared that thereafter in all matters of controversy relative to property and civil rights, resort should be had to the laws of England, as they stood in** 1792, **as the rule for the decision of the same, and shortly afterwards the criminal law of England was declared to be in force in the** Province. **Upon this grand foundation has the whole structure** of **Canadian institutions and Canadian** jurisprudence **been moulded and built.**

The Province was speedily divided into **great districts; courts were established,** officers were appointed, as in England ; and every provision **suitable** to a new country made for the conduct of affairs and the administration of justice. As early as 1797, the legal practitioners in the Province were incorporated, and the " **Law Society of Upper Canada** " established, as mentioned in the preamble to their Act of Incorporation, " **for the purpose of securing to the** Province and the profession a learned and honorable body, to assist their fellow **subjects as occasion** may require, and to support and maintain the constitution of the Province." *

In a new country those in authority naturally give the tone to morals, and impress their individuality on a people composed largely of the working classes; and for some thirty years settlements went on and the people prospered. These settlements were generally far apart, and the facilities for education very limited; but, as the country filled up, new districts were set apart with judicial, municipal, and educational organizations in each.

Until within the last fifty years, the country possessed comparatively few men properly qualified for taking part in public life, and many of the leading officials were men sent out from the Old Country.

But, as early as 1830, there was a change; and in 1840, when the two Provinces of Upper and Lower Canada were united under one Legislative Government, there was no ▸lack of competent men to supply the necessary positions, governmental, judicial, and ministerial, that the country required.

As already mentioned, Upper Canada was divided into districts, with distinct judicial establishments, and in 1842, with a resident Judge in each. Many of these districts were remote from the Seat of Government, not easy of access, and from the nature and general powers of the office and the isolated condition of the districts, the District Judge was necessarily an important character, not

* The Society has kept well abreast of the rapid progress of the Province, and has fully carried out its original aims. It is, perhaps, the best governed body, of its kind, in all Her Majesty's colonies.

merely in respect to his judicial functions, but because he was looked up to as the guide and leader in every movement for promoting the material good and well-being of the community. In fact, the design was, that he should be the exemplar of morals, and the guiding spirit in all progressive movements. The ability, energy, and example of the Judge, therefore, had much to do in giving a healthy tone to public opinion and effort before the days when railways, telegraphs, and the public press brought the people all over Canada into closer communication ; and hence, the recognized importance of having able men, energetic and strong of character, in the position of District Judges, and some fifty years ago ability and fitness were necessary passports to important offices. Those who can remember Upper Canada as it was fifty years ago, and look on the Canada of to-day, and, indeed, everyone acquainted with the history of the country, must be struck with the marvellous progress made within the last half century—progress in all that touches labor intelligently directed, in the forest, the field, the workshop, and the warehouse ; progress in all the material essentials for a healthy and happy existence. To secure and enjoy the fruit of their toil, men must have a settled government, wise laws rightly and duly administered, and an educated and progressive people. In this, also, and indeed in all the factors which go to build up national existence, solid progress has been made. These, and all these, are the outcome of individual influence and individual effort intelligently directed : and it is generally owing to the efforts of the few in these several fields that true and permanent progress is made in any community.

All honor to the toiling hand, and to the self-denying efforts of the husbandman, the artificer, the merchant, and others ; but let not the workers in other fields be forgotten, when we look with satisfaction on things as they are in our country, and contrast them with other countries, or with the primitive past. Those who assisted in any degree in the framing and development of Canadian laws and institutions deserve, at least, to be placed on the honor roll of our social history.

It is one of the men, who for more than fifty years of an unsullied life has been an earnest worker for his country in the line he had chosen—the Honorable Senator Gowan —of whom we purpose to speak, bringing together some particulars from various biographical and other sources* in relation to his career, and the progress to which he was an individual contributor.

The Honorable James Robert Gowan was born in Ireland, the 22nd December, 1815. He was the third son of Henry Hatton Gowan and Elizabeth, youngest daughter of Robert Burkitt, of Cahore.†

---

* "The Canadian Legal Biography," "Canadian Biographical Dictionary of Eminent Men," "Canadian Portrait Gallery," "Morgan's Canadian Directory," "Irishmen in Canada," "Cyclopedia of Canadian Biography," "Canadian Album of Men of Canada," "Prominent Men of Canada," and Illustrated and other Guides to the Senate of Canada—all of which contain biographical sketches of our subject : also, "Public Addresses presented to the Honorable J. R. Gowan, with gleanings from the press touching his career," compiled by a member of the Bar of Ontario, 1890.

† Robert Burkitt, of Cahore, belonged to a good old Lancashire family, as did his wife, Susannah Austin. Elizabeth, their daughter, was a remarkably clever woman, accomplished and well read in all the best literature of the

The lineage **and name of** Gowan are of the highest antiquity in Irish annals, and the tribal history reaches back to an early period in the Milesian records.[*]

Originally a powerful clan in Ulidia, in the twelfth century they were driven by the English into Donegal, and there, and in some of the adjoining counties, the chiefs of the clan settled and remained for centuries, with varied fortunes, and in the reigns of Henry VIII. and Elizabeth had mostly conformed to and accepted English rule.

In 1692, the Gowan family of Donegal divided into two branches—the younger remaining in Donegal ; the elder,

---

day ; and if, as has been said, talent comes from the mother, her son was well endowed. She had lost two boys in their infancy, and upon her only surviving son she exercised a most beneficial influence, cultivating his literary tastes, and forming and directing his strong character. Mr. Gowan always spoke of his mother with great veneration. She resided with him for over eleven years after he became Judge, and lived to an advanced age.

[*] According to O'Hart, the author of " Irish Pedigrees," "The Annals of the Four Masters," and earlier writers, the Gowan family is Milesian in origin, of the house of Ir of the Clan-na-Rory, and trace descent from a famous warrior of the Red Branch Knights of Ulster—Conall Cearnach, a near descendant of Ruadhri Mor, whose name appears on the roll of Milesian monarchs. From Conall Cearnach the chiefs of this clan, or family, have always maintained their descent, and in the annals of Irish history from an early period, and by the most reliable writers of ancient and modern times, has this claim been recognized. The clan, or tribe, originally called Gobhain, afterwards became known as O'Gowan, MacGowan, and Gowan, anglicized forms of an Irish word meaning armorer, or smith.

About the twelfth century the tribe were driven by the English into the county of Donegal, and Maurice MacGowan, of Bally Shannon, county of Donegal, a son of one of the chiefs of the clan, is the earliest ancestor of whom any certain detailed account remains. A record made by him in 1542 specifically sets forth the family descent from " Conall the Victorious," as then and now held.

represented by John Gowan, the great-great-grandfather of the subject of this memoir, becoming the head of the Leinster Gowans. But the direct recorded pedigree of the Honorable James R. Gowan extends back ten generations, to the latter part of the fifteenth century.*

John Gowan, of Lifford, Donegal, was one of those who opposed the rule of James II. in Ireland, and the principles he desired to force on the Irish people, and he played a part in the stirring events which led up to the change in dynasty. He became an officer in the army of William III., and served during the revolution, first in General Schomberg's division, and afterwards under General de Ginkle in his campaigns. He was present at the surrender of Limerick, and was one of those despatched to Dublin to announce the capitulation of that city.

---

* The general pedigree of the family, or tribe, is given by O'Hart in full. The direct pedigree from Maurice MacGowan to James Robert Gowan, of Ardraven, Barrie, in the Dominion of Canada, the last Gowan in his line of descent, is as follows :—

1. MAURICE MACGOWAN, *born* 1514; *mar.* JOAN O'DONNELL.
2. CONALL, his son, *born* 1540; *mar.* ROSE O'DONNELL.
3. PATRICK, his son, *born* 1566; *mar.* JANE ALLAN.
4. PHILIP GOWAN (who dropped the Mac in the family name), his son, *born* 1593; *mar.* ROSE DILLON.
5. THOMAS, the Rev., his son, *born* 1617; *mar.* MARY ST. LEGER.
6. THOMAS, the common ancestor of the Leinster and Ulster Gowans, his son, *born* 1642; *mar.* first, ANNE COOTE.
7. JOHN, his son by ANNE COOTE, *born* 1668; *mar.* MARTHA HUNTER.
8. JOHN HUNTER, his son, *born* 1699; *mar.* ANNE HATTON.
9. HENRY HATTON, his son, *born* 1736; *mar.* ANNE SMITH.
10. HENRY HATTON, his son, *born* 1778; *mar.* ELIZABETH BURKITT.
11. JAMES ROBERT GOWAN, the only son, was *born* 1815, and has no issue.

When the new dynasty was established John Gowan received a grant of land in Tipperary and married there. He had several sons who settled in Leinster, and acquired properties in the counties of Tipperary, Wexford, and Wicklow.

In the latter end of the last century, the descendants of John Gowan, the Leinster Gowans, were possessed of considerable landed estates in the counties named. Then followed the times when wild and reckless living and wanton extravagance prevailed amongst the landed classes in Ireland, and, as a natural consequence, the vicissitudes of families were rapid and startling, and, owing to a variety of causes, properties passed from the family or became hopelessly encumbered. Many younger members of the family left for other parts of the British Isles, and later on some emigrated to the Colonies or elsewhere ; many entered the army and navy, and the civil and military service in India ; and at this day it is believed the family has no representatives in the counties named.

Henry Hatton Gowan, the father of Senator Gowan, of Barrie, and the great-grandson of John Gowan, already named, had early determined on emigrating to Prince Edward Island, where a relation of his had been Governor,* but his son, being young, he remained in Ireland to secure a proper education for the lad, and he had the advantage

---

* This relation was Colonel Charles Douglas Smith, a relative of Mr. Gowan's mother, whose maiden name was Smith. Her father, *Charles Smith*, of Kyle, was a member of a rather celebrated family—that of the gallant Sir William Sidney Smith. General Edward Smith, Captain John Spencer Smith of the Guards, Gentleman Usher to Queen Charlotte and *Aide-de-Camp* to

of a sound education there, latterly under the Rev. Dr. Burnett, of Dublin, a well known educationalist of the day. In his sixteenth year the young man was actually placed with his maternal uncle, Dr. Robert Burkitt, to study medicine. But it was destined he should follow another course, and in a far off land.

In 1831 and 1832, the state of Ireland was most unsettled, life and property were considered insecure, everything was depressed, and the condition of things held out only the darkest prospects for the future of his family, so Mr. Gowan finally made up his mind to sell his property and emigrate to Canada with his family, which he accordingly did, sailing from New Ross in the spring of 1832.

The vessel the family sailed in was dismasted 1,000 miles from port, and had to return under jury-masts to Ireland for repairs ; but, after a second and protracted voyage, they at length arrived at Quebec, in the autumn of the same year, and at once proceeded to Upper Canada, their point of destination.

Mr. Gowan came to Canada with the intention of settling upon land in a good neighborhood, and, after spending nearly a year in quest of a desirable location, he finally purchased two adjoining farm properties in the township of Albion, not far from Toronto. He at once proceeded to erect better buildings and make necessary improve-

Lord George Sackville-Germain ; and Colonel Charles Douglas Smith, at one time Governor of Prince Edward Island. *Charles Smith* was the grandson of Edward Smith, who was brother to Captain Cornelius Smith, of Hythe, county of Kent. The latter was the great-grandfather of Sir William Sidney Smith and Colonel Charles Douglas Smith.

ments, and, having moved thereon with his family, he continued to reside there for some years. His son remained on the farm about a year, entering with enjoyment on a farm life in Canada. But the novelty soon wore off, and his father determined to put him to the profession of law rather than medicine, to which his parents had taken a dislike.*

Mr. Gowan accordingly placed his son as a student with a leading Toronto lawyer, the Honorable J E. Small, arranging with that gentleman that the young man should become a member of his family while studying under him for call to the Bar. In December, 1833, he was articled to Mr. Small as a student, and after the necessary term's notice, he subsequently appeared before the Benchers of the Law Society of Upper Canada, and, upon examination as to his fitness to enter on the study of the profession, was entered and ranked on the books of the Law Society as a student-at-law. From the first, and throughout his

---

* That the son himself had a decided taste for surgery and medicine is beyond a doubt. While a student in Toronto he induced his friends, Dr. Widmer and Dr. King, to take him to the Hospital, and he had frequent opportunities of seeing important operations there. As early as 1838, he became a subscriber to a medical journal, and in after years he was a regular reader of the leading medical periodicals, and followed carefully the advances in surgery and medicine. His first important case at the bar was the defence of a capital felony, where he found his medical reading of incalculable value. And the Judge has often said surgery and medicine was a necessary branch of legal education. For several years after the Judge entered on his duties, in some of the remote parts of his judicial district the people were thirty or forty miles from any medical practitioner. And it so happened that while on circuit and no doctor near, in several cases of accident and emergency, he was able to render aid to the sick or injured, in more than one case to the saving of life.

whole course as a student, Mr. Gowan was noted for diligence and attention to his studies, and was always conspicuous with his note book at every term and every sittings of the Courts. At Chambers he attracted the attention of two of the Judges, the late Sir John Beverley Robinson and the late Sir James Macaulay, both of whom, on many occasions, showed their appreciation of him, and after Mr. Gowan was appointed to the Bench the relations between him and these distinguished men continued to be of a very cordial character throughout their lives.

Mr. Gowan was an omnivorous reader and had marked literary tastes, and in the early part of his career in Toronto wrote a good deal. His attempts in a literary way were in contributions to " The Palladium," then owned and conducted by Mr. Fothergill, a prominent public man, and a well-known and able writer. He subsequently had a like connection with " The Patriot," owned by Robert Dalton, and with "The Examiner," started by Sir Francis Hincks, and later on was a contributor to English legal journals. His first effort in the way of law writing was in these. After a time he set to work in the preparation of an analytical index of the whole Statute law of Upper Canada, which he found very useful in Chambers, as it was the only complete index up to the time of its preparation. Subsequently, on a commission being appointed for the revision of the Statutes, he placed his manuscript at the disposal of Mr. John Hillyard Cameron, who was a member of the commission.

During the time Mr. Gowan was a student, occurred the rebellion of 1837. . A portion of the people had for

years alleged many and serious grievances touching **the**
administration of public affairs, and, under evil direction,
discontent culminated in open rebellion. The Governor,
momentarily expecting an attack, left the Government
House in Toronto, and occupied a central position in the
city, where a number of Loyalists congregated, and where
a quantity of arms was stored. There were no soldiers in
the Province at the time, and all Loyalists were called
upon to enrol themselves in defence of order and constitutional authority, and they quickly rallied round the representative of the Queen. Mr. Gowan was one of the first
to enrol his name and receive arms, and, with four or five
other law students, formed " The Governor's Body Guard '
at the city hall. When the body of Loyalists marched up
Yonge street to attack the rebels, Mr. Gowan was ordered
by the Colonel in command to join the left division, led
by Mr. Clark Gamble, a prominent barrister, and a gallant
gentleman,* and took part in the fight at " Gallow's Hill."

After the rebels were defeated, disaffection was thought
to prevail, and the militia were organized, and several
independent companies formed, amongst others, " The
Bank Guard," composed for the most part of bank officers,
law and medical students. This company supplied a regular nightly guard at the old Bank of Upper Canada, a
strong stone building, which was prepared to resist attack,
for there was deposited the money, as well as the important books and records of the Province. Many of the
young men who formed this guard, in after years occupied

* Mr. Gamble is still living.

the most important positions in the country. Senator
Gowan, Galt, C.J., Hagarty, C.J., and the Honorable
George Allan are the only survivors of this loyal band.
Mr. Gowan, shortly after the rebellion, received a commission in the Fourth North York Regiment of Militia, commanded by Charles Coxwell Small, Clerk of the Crown
and Pleas. But in those days there was little more than
an enrolment, and a few days' meeting in the year, of the
sedentary militia ; the volunteer system, which came in at
that time, being perfected at a later period. The old
Senator is rather proud of his commission, dated in 1838,
and retains the musket and accoutrements he carried in
the fight at Montgomery's Tavern.

It was a curious coincidence that, after the rebellion, he
was brought in contact with many of the men implicated
in the outbreak, some fifty or more of them having retained
the Honorable Mr. Small to defend them on charges of
treason and kindred offences. All the cases passed first
under the hands of Mr. Small's student, and this brought
him in constant personal contact with these men ; and
Mr. Gowan, as he often said in later years, was satisfied
that the great body of the men who attacked Toronto and
appeared in arms at Montgomery's, had no idea they were
committing an act of treason, but thought only of making
a strong political demonstration against the Government
of the day.

That many and great grievances existed, which were all
afterwards acknowledged and redressed, is a matter of history. The knowledge thus acquired had a great effect in
modifying Mr. Gowan's political views. Tory though he

was, by instinct and family traditions for centuries, he became an advocate for "responsible government," and what was then known as a "Baldwin Reformer." But he never had much interest in party politics; it was not in his line, and the only active part he ever took in politics was in the conduct of an election contest for his friend and partner, the Honorable Mr. Small, and in another election contest by the Honorable Mr. Baldwin.

Mr. Gowan, having passed with eclat the necessary final examinations, was called to the Bar in 1839, and at once connected himself in the practice of the law with the Honorable Mr. Small, having formed a partnership with that gentleman on an arrangement for an equal division of the profits from their practice. Mr. Small having devoted himself largely to public and political life, the general conduct of the business, including much of the counsel work, was cast almost entirely on Mr. Gowan, a formidable, as well as a responsible, task for a young man barely twenty-three years of age. He was a great worker, methodical and industrious, and carried on the business for nearly four years before his excellent constitution showed unmistakeable signs of inability to stand the strain. His health gave way. His intimate friend, brother mason,* and medical adviser, Dr. John King, of Toronto, advised him that only by an out-door life and greatly diminished mental work could his life be preserved and his health restored—a terrible outlook for a man of energy just entering on a career. This was in the latter part of 1842;

---

* The Senator became a member of St. Andrew's, No. 1, Toronto, in 1839, and has always been an ardent member of the order.

and just then it providentially happened that the very position to suit him in every way, as events proved, was placed at his disposal.

Some years previously an Act had been passed providing for the establishment of a new district—in addition to the nineteen into which Upper Canada was then divided, with judicial and municipal establishments in each—and on the erection and completion of the necessary public buildings, it was proclaimed under the name of the "District of Simcoe." Much sympathy was felt for Mr. Gowan by those he had come in contact with in the practice of his profession, and the Honorable Robert Baldwin, then Attorney-General, and a leading member of the Government of the day, spontaneously offered him the post of Judge of the new District of Simcoe.*

The salary was small, and the fees attached to the office uncertain as to amount, but under the law as it then stood, the incumbent was not debarred from counsel work at the Courts in Toronto. In the most favorable view, however, it meant a diminished income ; but, on the other hand, it gave promise of just the kind of regular out-door work which was a necessity to Mr. Gowan, and afforded scope for the exercise of his abundant energy. So he accepted the office—wisely, as it turned out for him, for he soon

---

* Mr. Dent, in his biographical work, suggests that possibly Mr. Gowan's partner in business being Solicitor-General, his influence may have secured the appointment for him. But such was not the case ; in fact, Mr. Small was unwilling to part with Mr. Gowan. The selection of Judge for the new district rested with the Honorable Mr. Baldwin, the Attorney-General, and the offer of the post came to Mr. Gowan from him alone.

recovered his health; happily for the district, which for many years derived the benefit of his valuable services.

A summary, which appeared some two years ago in a biographical sketch of Mr. Gowan, has suggested to us the order in which to treat more fully of the Honorable gentleman's public services, we therefore give it with a slight alteration to harmonize with our own method of treating the subject.

SUMMARY OF APPOINTMENTS HELD BY THE HONORABLE J. R. GOWAN, AND HIS PUBLIC SERVICES.

I.—JUDICIAL, viz :—

Appointed Judge of the Judicial District and Territories of Simcoe. Commission dated 17th January, 1843.

A continuous service of forty years (less six weeks)—as *sole Judge* over three distinct tribunals, civil and criminal, and *ex officio* Judge in Bankruptcy and in Insolvency, as well as over the several Division Courts in his Judicial District for some twenty-five years ; and afterwards as *Senior* Judge, with the assistance of a Deputy Judge, and Junior (or assistant) Judge, presiding over five distinct tribunals, a like continuous service of nearly fifteen years.

Appointed to the High Court of Justice for Ontario, March, 1882.

Retired from the Judicial office the end of October, 1883.

In 1884, re-appointed Chairman of the Board of Judges, the position being tenable by a retired Judge.

II.—Various duties and services in connection with all the Courts, and with procedure, under special delegation from the Executive, viz :—

1852.—Appointed, with four other Judges, to frame General Rules, etc., for the Division Courts.

1857.—Associated with Judges of Queen's Bench and Common Pleas in settling tariff of fees for the Profession and Officers of the Courts.

1858.—Appointed under statutory provision, with Chancellor Spragge and Justice Burns, to frame Rules of Procedure, etc., under the Act assimilating the law of Probate and Administration to that of England, and "for carrying the new law into beneficial effect."

1869.—Appointed Chairman of the Board of five Judges, commissioned to make orders touching procedure, and to settle conflicting decisions of the Division Courts.

1871.—Appointed on the Commission of Judges, Chief Justice Wilson, Chairman, to enquire into the Constitution and Jurisdiction of the several Courts of law and equity in Ontario, with a view to "fusion of law and equity."

III.—Designated by special appointment for extraordinary and peculiar judicial service, viz :—

1862.—Appointed Chairman and acted as Judicial Referee, with Experts, in taking evidence and in determining the differences between the Government of Canada and the several contractors respecting the erection of the Public and Parliamentary Buildings at Ottawa.

1873.—Appointed and acted on the Royal Commission of three Judges empowered to investigate certain charges made in Parliament against Cabinet Ministers in connection with the Canadian Pacific Railway contract.

IV.—Services outside the judicial duties proper of his office.

Largely engaged in the work of Revision and Consolidation of the Statutes, civil and criminal, viz :—

1st. The Statutes of Upper Canada, from 32nd George III. to 22nd Victoria.

2nd. The Statutes of Canada, up to 1859.

3rd. In the preparation of the several Criminal Law Acts of 1869.

4th. The Ontario Consolidation of 1877.

V.—Work and assistance in the preparation of technical matter touching Legislative improvements—work which **in** England is done by official draftsmen and paid experts— Mr. Gowan, at the instance of the Law Officers of the Crown and under different administrations, for over thirty years was so engaged, as the following outline will show, viz :—

Under the Honorable Robert Baldwin :
> In relation to the Municipal **System : Division** Courts and Magistrate's Law.

Under the Honorable Sir William Richards :
> In relation to the Criminal Law : The local Courts, Civil and Criminal procedure, etc.

Under the **Honorable John** Sandfield McDonald :
> In relation to procedure in the Courts, and summary **Criminal procedure.**

Under Sir John A. Macdonald :
> In relation to the Criminal Law : The Common Law Procedure for the Superior and local Courts, in conjunction with Chief Justice Draper ; in the preparation of the Crown Prosecutor and **C. J.** Criminal Court system.
>
> The assimilation of the law of Probate and Administration to the English system.
>
> The improvement and extension of the Local Courts system, and in the preparation of numerous measures in relation to the Law, civil and criminal, and its administration during the whole time Sir John Macdonald was Attorney-General for Canada, and Minister of Justice for the Dominion.

This summary shows an extensive ground to cover, even with an outline treatment, yet we hope to leave no important matter untouched, and proceed with our subject in the order just given.

Mr. Gowan's commissions as Judge of the Courts, civil and criminal, are dated 17th January, 1843. He was a young Judge, but as remarked by the author of the Cyclopedia of Canadian Biography, "No tribute is needed from any pen to the legal capabilities and integrity of a young man whom the Honorable Robert Baldwin would select at the age of twenty-five to fill a place upon the Bench.

Note.—Statement, in order of date, of the chief commissions and appointments held by Senator Gowan, and those in connection with his public services :—

1834.—Admitted, upon examination, to the Law Society of Upper Canada.

1837.—Joined the Loyalists at the City Hall, Toronto, on the breaking out of the Rebellion. Enrolled for duty and served as a volunteer in the fight with rebels at Gallows Hill.

1837.—Enrolled a member of "The Bank Guard."

1838.—Commissioned as Ensign in "The Fourth North York Militia."

1839.—Appointed Lieutenant, same regiment, Lieutenant-Colonel C. C. Small commanding.

1839.—Called to the degree of Barrister of Law, having passed the necessary examinations.

1843.—Appointed to the Judicial Office ; commission dated 17th January.

1843.—Appointed to Board of Trustees of Barrie Grammar School.

1844.—Appointed Chairman of "The Board of Public Instruction" for Simcoe, which position he held until 1871, when the system was changed.

1854.—Appointed on Commission of Judges empowered to make Rules for Division Courts.

1857.—Appointed, in association with Judges of Courts at Toronto, to devise and settle the Fees to be taken by Officers and Practitioners of the Courts.

Such appointments are rare if not altogether exceptional in our judicial history."

The new District of Simcoe, to which Mr. Gowan was appointed the first, and it may be well said the pioneer, Judge, embraced a very large territory bordering on Lakes Huron and Simcoe, extending northward some 200 miles to the French River, while its southern boundary was

---

1858.—Appointed, with Chancellor Spragge and Justice Burns, to frame Rules of Procedure under the Statutes relating to Guardianship, Probate and Administration, and for carrying the new law into beneficial effect.

1858.—Appointed, with C. J. Sir James Macaulay, to revise and consolidate the whole body of the Statute Law of Upper Canada ; and in

1859.—In association with G. W. Wickstead, Law Clerk, and Sir J. Macaulay, the Statute Law of Canada ; and later on, in

1859.—With both the gentlemen named, in the work of interpolation of the Acts of the Session, for proclamation in November of that year.

1862.—Appointed as Judicial Referee, and acted as Chairman, in the determination of the differences between the Government of Canada and the contractors for the erection of the Public and Parliamentary Buildings at Ottawa.

1869.—Appointed Chairman of the Board of Judges commissioned to make Rules of Procedure for the Division Courts, and to settle conflicting decisions.

1869.—Assisted in the drafting and preparation of the several Criminal Law Bills and Consolidation, introduced in Parliament by Sir John Macdonald, the Premier and Minister of Justice, which passed and became law.

1871.—Appointed on the Commission of Judges, of whom C. J. Wilson was Chairman, to enquire into the Constitution and Jurisdiction of the several Courts of Law and Equity in Ontario, with a

within thirty miles of Lake Ontario, and the city of
Toronto. It contained between twenty and thirty settled
or partially settled townships, averaging ten miles square
each, and much unsurveyed territory, including the districts of Muskoka and Parry Sound, and the islands in
Lakes Huron and Simcoe lying opposite the district. The
chief town, Barrie, the seat of the Courts and the place
where the public buildings were erected, is beautifully

---

view to fusion of Law and Equity; and with Judges Gwynne
and Patterson, afterwards of the Supreme Court, drafted Bill
for the purpose.

1873.—Appointed one of the three Judges on the Royal Commission
empowered to investigate charges against Cabinet Ministers in
connection with the Canadian Pacific Railway contract.

1877.—Appointed by the Government of Ontario, with other Judges, on
the Commission for the Consolidation of the whole Statute
Law of the Province.

1881.—Appointed Chairman of the Board of the Barrie Collegiate-Insti-
tute, an office he held, by annual election and appointment,
until his resignation in 1892.

1882.—Appointed to the High Court of Justice for Ontario, his commission as Judge dated 14th March of that year.

1883.—Re-appointed Chairman of the Board of Judges by the Government of Ontario, the position being tenable by a retired Judge.

1884.—The degree of LL.D. conferred upon him by the University of
Queen's, Kingston.

1885.—Summoned to the Upper House, and became a Senator of
Canada.

1889.—Appointed Queen's Counsel by Government of Canada.

1890.—Admitted to King's Inn and called to the Irish Bar.

1892.—The Queen conferred upon him the dignity of C.M.G., "in
recognition of his long and valuable services to the State."

situated on an arm of **Lake Simcoe**; indeed **the whole** region **is** strikingly attractive and picturesque.*

The settlements were scattered and, **in some cases, far apart, and** connected only **by** forest roads, pleasant for **riding on** horseback and suitable enough for sleighing in **winter,** but almost impassable for carriages of any kind in **Spring and Autumn. But the new** district was then the **largest settled territorial and judicial district in the Pro- vince, and the large area of fertile land it contained and its water facilities gave ample promise of large and rapid** increase.†

---

* A former Governor General, Sir John Colborne, much favored the terri- tory around Lake Simcoe as a place for settlement, and induced many retired officers of the army and navy to take up their land grants there. Several of the townships, West Gwillimbury, Tecumseth, Innisfil, Essa, Mono, and Adjala, were settled largely by emigrants direct from the British Isles; and two other large townships were first settled by Gælic-speaking people from the Highlands and islands of Scotland. To the north, on Lake Huron, the townships were settled chiefly by French, from Lower Canada. This was especially so around Penetanguishene, a very old and important naval and military station on Lake Huron, which continued to be occupied by Imperial troops for several years after 1842.

† This hope was amply fulfilled, for, within a generation, two new counties were carved out of it, and later on two judicial districts, with judicial, muni- cipal, and educational institutions in each, so rapid was the growth in popula- tion. Judge Gowan, in his valedictory to the Bar in 1883, referred to this. "As you are aware," said he, "this is the largest judicial district in the country, its population not long since being equal to that of the Provinces of Manitoba and British Columbia together," and its marvellous progress in other particulars could well be enlarged upon. When Judge Gowan, in January, 1843, came to the district there were some four resident ministers of the Church of England, now there are at least twenty-two. It certainly did not contain more than ten public schools, and was without a single grammar

The whole judicial duties and the exercise of large, general powers in this extensive district, were then entrusted to a single officer, who presided over all its tribunals, superior and inferior, civil and criminal, and had certain appellate jurisdiction in matters of local administrators, as well as the sole power of appointment and removal of officers for his Courts. And the District Judge was, moreover, expected to take part in honorary duties connected with education, and to co-operate, if not

---

school, while now, even in its reduced area, there are over 150 good public schools, with suitable school house and proper equipments for each, all provided with legally qualified teachers. And so with regard to grammar schools, there are now four, each with handsome and suitable buildings (one a collegiate institute), with a full complement of masters—graduates; and in this connection may be mentioned a number of mechanics' institutes and public libraries, regulated and partly supported by the State.

In 1843, the district was served by some thirty post offices; now the postal service includes over 230 offices, with an inspector at the chief town, assisted by a full staff of subordinates. As to public roads, there was then not fifty miles of really good road in all the district, and communication was difficult, and often dangerous; now, north, south, east and west, the district is netted over by railways, with a regular passenger service of eight trains daily throughout the year, and full and complete daily freight service. The same development is to be recorded with regard to water communication. In 1843, two small steamers and a few schooners were sufficient to do the carrying trade of the people of the district bordering on these inland seas, while now hundreds of vessels find full employment, and, on Lake Huron, two navigation companies are fully and profitably engaged, each with a fine fleet of well appointed steamers engaged in the mercantile service, at the ports of Collingwood, Meaford, Penetanguishene, Midland, Parry Sound and other ports in the district, to which also there is a large resort of foreign vessels, employed chiefly in the lumber trade. One further evidence of increase may be mentioned— namely, in the public journals—from one single newspaper, in the early days of the district, to over twenty well conducted local newspapers.

lead, in every movement for the advancement of the moral and material good of the people.

In view of all this, an educated, able man, a man of force of character, as well as ability, was required, and it was generally considered that a high compliment was paid Mr. Gowan, when he was selected by so cautious and conscientious a statesman as the Honorable Robert Baldwin, to fill the position.

In accepting the judgeship offered to him by Mr. Baldwin, Mr. Gowan did not surrender his business connection with Mr. Small, but the firm was increased by an additional partner, Mr. John Strathy, a Scotch lawyer, who had been recently called to the Bar of Upper Canada, and was subsequently married to Mr. Gowan's younger sister.

Mr. Gowan visited Toronto occasionally for counsel work, doing a good deal in the way of drafting at home ; but this lasted little more than two years, for an alteration in the law properly prevented resident judges from practice of any kind.*

Immediately after his appointment Mr. Gowan came to his district, and was in a short time followed by his

---

* The office at that day was somewhat similar to that of a Judge in the old principality of Wales.

Some two years after his appointment, as has been said, an Act was passed taking away entirely the right to practice as counsel. At that time Mr. Gowan had a lucrative connection with the law firm of "Small, Gowan & Strathy," Barristers, Toronto, the Honorable J. E. Small, Solicitor-General, being the head. The compensation allowed did not equal one-fourth of his professional income from outside practice. Other Judges in like case, with no means except their judicial salaries, were driven to resignation. Mr. Gowan was not so circumstanced, and continued in office. As the late Premier

family, his father, Mr. Henry Hatton Gowan, having received the appointment of Clerk of the Crown for the district, which was held by him up to the time of his decease. The new Judge at once entered on the duties of the office and the necessary organization in the newly constituted district. The co-operation of the local magistracy was necessary in the matter of organization, and the new Judge unfortunately found a determination to block him in every way, even in the approving of the securities of the High Sheriff and other officers, and in assigning territorial limits for the Division Courts. A change of Government had recently taken place, and to the Baldwin-Lafontaine Government, then in power, the magistrates almost without exception, were bitterly opposed.

Moreover, some who had expected official appointments were dissappointed. At all events so it happened that the young Judge instead of receiving the co-operation he had a right to expect from the resident magistrates, met only bitter opposition, and personal hostility, carried even into social matters in some cases. After making many efforts at conciliation, without effect, the Judge determined on submitting a drastic course of action to the Government to enable the district to be properly organized, at the same time placing his resignation of office in the

---

of Canada remarked, "It was fortunate for the country that he did, for he had time to prepare laws as well as to administer them."

The prohibition of outside practice by one holding an important judicial position was, no doubt, a proper provision in itself. But it was a breach of faith to alter the conditions under which individuals accepted office, without providing just compensation.

hands of the Government in case they were not disposed to accept his suggestion. This was to supersede the whole Commission of the Peace and issue a new one, containing only three or four names suggested by him, on whose aid he could rely in carrying out certain statutory provisions. The suggestion was accepted, the Government taking care to place the responsibility of the act on the Judge. A new commission was issued to the Judge himself; Colonel Irving, the appointee of the Crown, for the office of District Warden; Captain Elms Steele, R. N., the member representing a portion of the district, and to Mr. George Lount, Registrar of Deeds for the district. With the co-operation of these gentlemen the Judge at once put the business in proper shape; had the district divided into Court divisions and shortly after appointed all the officers necessary for the new Courts. Within a few months, the whole civil and criminal organization in the district was complete and in good working order. Mr. Gowan took early occasion to visit every part of his extensive jurisdiction, and lost no opportunity, as became a pioneer Judge, in impressing upon all the necessity of aiding the authorities in the discharge of their official duties and in inculcating obedience to the law, as the only safeguard of life, liberty and property, addressing the people on every proper occasion, especially on his circuits at the opening of each Court. He took much pains to impress on people, who in some of the settlements had hitherto lived almost out of reach of legal restraint, the value of settled institutions and British law.

After some time, on the Judge's recommendation, a new

Commission of the Peace for the district was issued, which contained the names of the magistrates who had been superseded under the temporary commission, as well as a considerable number of new men in whom the inhabitants had confidence. Upon these latter a dead set was made by some of the old magistrates, and the Judge felt it became him to give them every instruction as to their duties and powers, and to assist them in every way to rightly perform these duties ; and notwithstanding the watchful and hostile espionage to which their every act was exposed, no valid objection could be found to their action. After a time the old magistrates, with two or three exceptions, became reconciled and took the necessary oaths under the new commission.

It can be easily understood that the magistracy in a young community needed all the assistance possible, and this the Judge voluntarily rendered, notwithstanding the onerous duties incumbent upon him as a pioneer Judge in the organization of a new district.

After the district had been fully organized, and all the courts and municipal and other institutions were in good working order, the magistrates of the district, sensible of the Judge's efforts in the public interests, determined on a souvenir of their appreciation, and presented him with a valuable snuff-box of exquisite workmanship in gold, of three colors, on which the following was engraved :—
" Presented to His Honor James Robert Gowan by the Magistrates of the District of Simcoe, who gratefully acknowledge his invaluable services in the judicial organization of this new district, and his uniform kindness to them personally."

By this time the young Judge had become well-known
all over the district ; he had succeeded in overcoming
many and discouraging obstructions, had acquired the
confidence of the leading inhabitants, in fact, made an
excellent start in the work of a pioneer Judge, as well as
contributing to educational and municipal progress. As
he wrote to a friend some three years after his appointment, " I have now a pretty full acquaintance with my
surroundings ; I like the work, with all its labors and
responsibilities, and there is now only plain sailing before
me ; my health is excellent, and I hope, please God, to do
a grand work here, and build up a good record as a pioneer Judge." He did so, and he and his many friends
have the pleasure of looking back, with satisfaction, on
nearly half a century of continuous, useful labor in the
public service.

From the first he was untiring and energetic, and
labored under difficulties, which no longer exist, in the
performance of his judicial work. In all the great district
the Judge presided over there were not fifty miles of what
could be called good road, while some of his Courts were
over one hundred miles apart, and travel had to be on
horseback or by sleighing in the winter.* The Judge rode

* The few clergymen of the Church of England in the district had extensive
missions in connection with their parishes, that of Barrie some hundred miles
in extent, the incumbent's then field of labor being now divided into fifteen
or sixteen parishes. In consequence of the remoteness of settlements, and the
dangers of travel, the missionary could not make more than two rounds in the
year—one in summer, the other in winter ; and the rector of Barrie, or his
curate, were only too glad to select the time of Judge Gowan's circuits, and to
have the advantage of his arrangements for travelling through the forest. It

well, kept excellent horses, and was able to get over the
ground rapidly, and sixty to eighty miles in a day was no
uncommon ride with him ; and he has often boasted that,
though considered a hard rider, he had never broken down
a horse. In the winter the travelling was somewhat dangerous, not to speak of the long exposure with the thermometer below zero, and the Judge had several very
narrow escapes from death in his travels through the new
country. He was often compelled literally to take his
life in his hands in the course of his official peregrinations.
He was always exposed to dangers from which travellers
in the rural districts in Canada are not altogether free
even at the present day—such dangers, for instance, as
damp beds, unwholesome and ill-cooked food, and badly
ventilated rooms. This was the case, especially in the
western portion of his district, for there the settlements
were isolated, with forest stretches between them, and
only one or two houses where shelter could be obtained.
One of these, a rude log hut, some fifteen by twenty feet,
was occupied by an old man named Brock and his wife.
For some years after 1843, new townships to the west
were being opened for sale and settlement, and hundreds
of settlers who were pouring in to take up farms frequently
sought the shelter of Brock's house. On one or two occa-

commonly happened that, after the Judge's Court was concluded, the Church
service was held in the Court room, many of those who had attended the
Court remaining. The settlers for a considerable distance round attended
these services, the Old Country folk being conspicuous with their prayer books.
It was only on these rare occasions that they were able to have the rites of
their Church, and it was no uncommon thing to see a whole family of children
baptized together.

sions the Judge found this small building so full of these
wayfarers, that at night they covered the floor, lying closely
together before the huge wood fire, but the Judge had a
bed improvised for him by poles inserted in the log walls ;
with the thermometer below zero, even this rude shelter
was not to be despised. On several other occasions the
Judge, unable to reach any house, had to bivouac in the
snow, and with his sleigh upturned and pine branches to
keep off the wind, wrapped in buffalo robes, he passed the
night as best he could.*

But snow or storm, rain or heat, never prevented him
keeping his Court appointments; nor was his travel always
without personal danger from other causes, for a somewhat lawless condition existed in portions of his district,
where the settlers, up to the time of his coming, were
almost without any legal restraint, and to these places the
Judge did not go unprepared to defend himself. But only
on two occasions was personal encounter forced upon him
—his assailants only were the sufferers—but of these early
episodes he was always most unwilling to speak. While
on circuit through the district, settlers everywhere in these
primitive days came to him for advice in local and family
troubles, and many a feud was averted or healed, many a .
family difficulty set right by his wise and judicious suggestions and interference.

Besides the circuit work there were four Court sittings
yearly held at the district town, lasting from one to two
weeks each, for disposal of the civil and criminal business

---

* "Canadian Portrait Gallery," and other papers.

with the assistance of Grand and Petit jurors, and these occasions, especially in the early years of his advent were seized on by the Judge as occasions for timely instruction and information.

In time the district grew to be a model one in the orderly arrangement of its Courts and otherwise, and the Judge came to have the advantage of a very able Bar, with whom his relations were of the most agreeable character.

Mr. Gowan at the time of his appointment had barely three years and six months standing at the Bar,* and, as noticed in the public journals of the day, was the youngest man ever entrusted with Her Majesty's commission as a Judge, either in England or the Colonies. He consequently brought all the energy and vigor of youth to the discharge of his judicial functions, and the multitudinous duties incident to the position of a District Judge, and all his great working powers were needed. Through his whole life, and up to recent date, he was an early riser, and as he himself often said to friends, the best part of his day's work was done in his library before most people were out of their beds.

He brought with him a large and well selected library of general and professional works, and he took in all the leading legal periodicals ; indeed for several years his was the only good law library in the district, and it was always open for use to the members of the profession. Though he was a great and persistent reader, yet only in cases of

---

* A few years after, a standing of five years at the Bar was made a necessary qualification for the judicial office.

emergency did he allow his reading to encroach on his regular hour for retiring.

His father, who as before mentioned, was appointed Clerk of the Crown and Pleas for the Judicial District, with his mother and unmarried sister* went to Barrie with him, and so the Judge was saved from thought about domestic concerns, and was thus able to give his whole time and attention to the duties of his office, and to those public concerns in which he was engaged. And so it continued after his marriage, for in 1853, Mr. Gowan married Anne, second daughter of the Rev. S. B. Ardagh, A.M., rector of Barrie,† and this most estimable lady and his father, who lived many years after his son's marriage, were ever solicitous to leave him no anxiety about home matters, and though the Judge exercised an abundant hospitality nothing was allowed to interfere with his time or employments. His position, was therefore, most favorable for work, and those who knew him in these days used to say, "he was never idle, and never seemed in a hurry, except when on horseback."

---

* This was his eldest sister, Anne, who, in 1846, married Dr. John Russell Ardagh, A.B., T.C.D.; both dead for some years. Their only son, Henry Hatton Ardagh, Barrister, married Marcia, only daughter of Colonel N. H. Fishe, R.A., and has issue. His younger sister, Susannah Elizabeth, had married John Strathy, Barrister, and their eldest son, John Alexander Strathy, married Agnes Strachan, youngest daughter of the Very Reverend Dean Grasett, M.A., and has issue. Mrs. Strathy was a few years younger than her brother. She died recently, to his great grief.

† Mr. and Mrs. Gowan lately celebrated the forty-first anniversary of their wedding day. Mrs. Gowan is the worthy helpmeet of her talented husband, being widely known and esteemed for her sweet and active Christian life and her abundant charity.

Of Judge Gowan's excellence as a Judge and his work generally, much might be said, and the biographer has ample material from which to select opinions and eulogiums upon his judicial ability. A few will be given, which may be prefaced by an expression from one who knew Judge Gowan well : " His fearless honesty was only equalled by his industry, and produced a confidence almost without parallel in all his decisions. This, the fact that appeals from his decisions were almost unknown, abundantly proves, seeing that he acted in the presence of a large and able Bar, and amongst an intelligent people, tenacious of their rights" The letters to him from the leading Judges after his retirement show how correct were the remarks quoted, and lend emphasis to them. For example ; the late Chief Justice of Ontario, Sir Adam Wilson, said : "Your decisions were very rarely up in appeal, the best evidence that they were sound and satisfactory. I do not know if any of them have been overruled, and, if they had, it would not have been an infallible test of their unsoundness." Sir William Richards, late Chief Justice of the Supreme Court, wrote in the same strain to Mr. Gowan : "After a man has worked as hard and as faithfully as you have done for more than forty years, he has the right to seek relaxation. You may properly feel proud not only of your able and energetic discharge of judicial duty, well warranting the reputation you obtained for sound judgment and efficient service, but also for the voluntary and patriotic aid you were willing and able to lend public men in preparing and revising measures of law reform, as I very well know."

The late Chancellor Spragge, then Chief Justice of the Court of Appeal, wrote : " We are both veterans in the public service, you with a judicial life longer than mine. You retire with the regret of those you leave behind. I hope sincerely you may enjoy your *otium cum dignitate*, for a long time. You certainly have earned retirement, if long, and efficient, and valuable services can entitle any man to it."

Mr. Justice Gwynne, of the Supreme Court, also wrote of Mr. Gowan's " long and distinguished labors in discharge of his official duties." " Few men," he said, " can look back with equal satisfaction on the useful and varied labors of their life." The late Sir Matthew Cameron, C.J.C.P., after Mr. Gowan's appointment to the Senate, wrote : " Moulding laws, as well as expounding them, I hope, may form not an uncongenial pursuit, and that you may derive some pleasure in the passing of laws as the country derived benefit from your able exposition of them on the Bench, during a long tenure of office."

Sir Alexander Campbell, Minister of Justice for the Dominion, on the occasion of Mr. Gowan's retirement, wrote expressing his hearty approval of the complimentary remarks in the Order-in-Council accepting Mr. Gowan's resignation. " For over forty years the country has had the benefit of your faithful service, in the honorable position you adorned, and you have well earned your retirement." The Right Honorable Sir John Macdonald, late Premier of Canada, in referring to the terms of this Order-in-Council, wrote, " You will see there a just tribute to your long and faithful judicial services. So far as I know, this is the only instance in which such a testimony has been given to any Judge of any Court, but you have well earned the thanks of the Government and the community." To this we would add two notices which appeared in the "Canada Law Journal," in October and November, 1883 : "As we go to press, we notice the retirement of His Honor James Robert Gowan. * * Those only, and the circle of these is no limited one, who know of his learning, his large and ripened experience, and his great service to the country in numberless ways, can measure the loss this will be to the Bench, of which he was *facile princeps*. * * Judge Gowan occupies as strong a position in the hearts of his friends and acquaintances, from his high personal character, as from his judicial excellence. A kind thoughtfulness for others, and a benevolent disposition, endeared him to the community in which he has heretofore passed his long and useful life. Spotless purity, entire freedom from undue influence, and an earnest desire to do justice, have characterized him as a Judge. Great force of character, combined with cordiality and courtesy of demeanour, and a high consideration for the performance of his duties, have distinguished him as a citizen. * * He takes with him into his well earned retirement, the best wishes of a large circle of friends and admirers for his future health and happiness ; and we trust that, in some way or another, the country may still have the benefit of his ripe experience. His career is a brilliant example to those who occupy similar positions of trust and dignity, to emulate which will be a duty, and to equal which will indeed be difficult."

* * "We believe, that throughout the whole of his judicial career but two of his judgments were reversed. * * All of his judgments that we have read are clear in diction, dignified and concise, * * entirely free from any parade of learning or affectation ; two objects seemed to absorb the attention of the Judge, (1) properly to adjust the disputed rights of the parties ; (2) to establish a rule by which similar questions may be solved in the future, and if possible to bring each case within the scope of some general principle which he had enunciated and defined, guarding it, however, with proper conditions and exceptions. * * The soundness of his judgments and the care with which he prepared his decisions is evinced by the fact, before mentioned, that but two of his judgments appear to be reversed on appeal."

No more complete testimony could be given to judicial excellence than that borne in the letters from the distinguished writers above quoted. But Mr. Gowan had other duties besides those of a Judge sitting in Term, or with a jury in the trial of cases in the Superior Courts in his district at the chief town, from which there was an appeal. He acted also as Judge of the Division Courts scattered over the district, with power of summary decision upon the law and fact, and that without appeal. This portion of a pioneer Judge's duty in a new district was of great importance, for where everything is in a transition state in a partially settled country, there is usually much friction and frequent conflict, and consequently much litigation, the cases commonly contentious and in most instances conducted by the parties themselves, without legal assistance. Their claims for debt or damages might be relatively small, but were felt by the parties concerned to be of paramount interest, and were so in fact to them. And here came in an important function in a pioneer Judge to decide aright according to law and good conscience, at the same time explaining and vindicating the wisdom of the law as occasion arises, so as to satisfy all, if possible, that justice was done. And herein it was that Judge Gowan's quick perception and marvellous knowledge of human nature was conspicuous, and secured for him the unbounded confidence of litigants.*

He acted on the principle that "the concerns of these Courts could not be regarded as small, the principles of justice made them great," and however inconsiderable the amount involved, every case received his best consideration. And in the early days of his career many thousand such cases came before him. His great pleasure was to

---

* "We learn from older members of the Bar that there never was a feeling in this judicial district that 'it depended upon the humor of the Judge what character the law assumed.' So far from that, every practitioner felt confidence in advising his client, upon ascertained facts, what the decision would probably be. This was a matter of great importance in those days when the bulk of the law business was done in the Division Courts, and when there was no appeal from the decision of the Judge acting in these Courts, though retained in the other Courts over which he presided. The feeling of confidence and certainty to which we refer, was conspicuous very early in Judge Gowan's judicial life, and in this connection may be given the language of an address, presented to him in 1852, by the magistrates, councillors and others, residents of the western townships, after a new district was set off from the territory then in his jurisdiction, and formed into the District of Grey. The address speaks of the manner in which the duties in the particular Court for the locality had been performed: 'and the usefulness of that Court, under your Honor's

get them amicably settled when cases originated in family disputes, so as to avoid bringing out matters that might leave incurable wounds—and, indeed, often without any suit at all, parties came to him at his lodgings after Court, or stopped him on the highway to induce him to pass upon their differences, which he generally did, giving his views as to what was just, and almost invariably it was accepted, and in this way many difficulties were settled that would otherwise have entered into litigation.

As population increased new districts with their own separate judicial and municipal establishments were carved out of the District of Simcoe, but business transactions expanding and becoming more important, and the duties in the higher Courts demanding more of his time in the chief town, the Judge had occasionally to avail himself of the services of a Deputy Judge in the Division Courts. The increased work made it absolutely necessary there should be a permanent increase in the judiciary of the

---

jurisdiction, in giving soundness to pecuniary transactions, confidence in commercial affairs, and a high tone of moral feeling;' and adds 'on your separation from this division, in taking leave of you, we beg to assure you that it is with mingled feelings of respect and regret; respect for you as an able and upright Judge, and regret that we have lost your valuable services.' Referring to this address, the 'Barrie Herald,' of 7th April, 1852, says, amongst other things: 'From personal attendance for a period of more than six years at many of the Courts over which Judge Gowan presides, we are warranted in expressing our conviction that to his integrity, ability, and painstaking efforts, and not merely to the value of the system itself, may be traced the existence of the order of things fitly described in the address to him as "giving soundness to pecuniary transactions, confidence in commercial affairs, and a higher tone to moral feeling," throughout the country.'"—"Career of Judge Gowan," by a member of the Bar, 1890.

District, and in 1872, Mr. John A. Ardagh was appointed by the Crown a junior or assistant resident Judge. Though a graduate of Trinity College, he had received his primary education at the Barrie grammar school. He was a son of the rector of Barrie, and a brother-in-law of Judge Gowan, and there is little doubt Sir John Macdonald consulted the Judge on the appointment of his colleague, as well as on the previous appointment in 1858, of Mr. William D. Ardagh,* the Deputy Judge in the district.

Mr. John Ardagh's appointment was an excellent one ; he had the vigor of youth on his side and an excellent standing at the Bar.† But even with the increased judicial power, the work was very large, and Judge Gowan retained in his own hands the power of appointment and removal of officers of the Courts. Much of the value of the Division Courts, which are somewhat similar to the English County Courts, depended upon the efficiency and integrity of the subordinate officers, and the Judge had exercised great judgment in their selection, taking a good deal of trouble in instructing them by word and occasional " papers."

That he was eminently successful in obtaining good and reliable men for the office is proved by the fact that of

---

* Mr. William D. Ardagh afterwards entered public life, and became a member of the Legislature. He subsequently went to Manitoba, where he became Deputy Attorney-General, and was afterwards appointed a District Judge in that Province, which office he held at the time of his death.

† Mr. Ardagh is now the Senior Judge, with Mr. William Boys, the Assistant or Junior Judge.

over one hundred officers appointed by him, against four
only was sufficient cause for their removal shown.*

In connection with the judicial office, a good deal of
work of a general character outside the Judge's particular
Court came to him in the regulation of details of procedure
in the various tribunals of justice, civil and criminal, of

---

* " Perhaps the most striking evidence of his great aptitude for the position,
was his wise and successful administration of patronage, in the selection of
officers for the several Division Courts over which he presided. Until very
recently, the duty of appointing all the officers of these Courts belonged to the
Senior Judge—the power of appointment and removal—for all held office
during the pleasure of the Judge. In Judge Gowan's extended jurisdiction he
had the appointment to some twenty-five offices, several of them, at the time,
giving an income, from fees, larger than the Judge's own salary. During the
whole period of his incumbency, over one hundred officers were appointed by
him, and so judicious had been his selection that only four men of his appointment were removed for misconduct or neglect in the long period of forty years.
The other changes that occurred in that time were due to resignation, removal
or death. A few years ago an ex-M.P., who spoke ' from actual knowledge,
having resided in the county longer than the Judge himself, and somewhat
intimately acquainted with public feeling,' in a letter published at the time,
refers to the Judge's administration, in this particular, as ' a matter which
has deservedly, long since, obtained the approbation of thinking men of all
parties in this community, namely, the wise and just manner in which, for over
a third of a century, the Judge has exercised the large patronage vested in
his office ;' and in proof, mentions a fact to show how well officers of his
appointment stood with the public. He says : ' No less than eight were
elected reeves, and some of them re-elected again and again, and three served
in the honorable office of warden, with several others, chosen to fill the office
of councillors in local municipalities,' and he might have added, more than
one elected to the Legislature. In commenting on this the ' Advance ' newspaper says : ' It may seem a simple thing to many, to choose always the best
men for such positions, but such a choice requires two things, and these two
the Judge possessed in a singular degree. The first, an insight into character,
a capability of judging what a man really *was* no matter what he *seemed to be*.

the country. To secure the effectual working of statutory
provisions, the Legislature delegates to the Executive the
power to select a certain number of Judges, to frame rules
and regulations touching procedure, the remuneration by
fees to executive officers of the Courts. And these rules
and regulations in amplification of statutory provisions

It has been remarked, even by some who grudgingly conceded praise to those
who differed from them, that the Judge possessed in a most remarkable way, the
faculty of reading character, and of detecting the secret workings that animated
those, whose actions and motives it was necessary that he should discover and
understand. He could at once gauge a man, and, as the result generally
showed, correctly. The other faculty required, as to such appointments, is
the courage to appoint the best man, once he was found, despite the many
adverse influences brought to bear. 'The public good' was, in an essential
manner, Judge Gowan's motto. We have before us a 'paper' issued by
him to officers of his Division Courts some years ago, and we make one
extract which will serve to show how he exercised the patronage reposed in
him."

"'The letter of the Statute makes the tenure of office, for both clerk and
bailiff, during the *pleasure* of the Judge ; but an office connected with the
administration of justice ought, at least practically, to be upon a more certain
tenure—and while willing and able to do the duties required of him faithfully,
discreetly, and in the mode prescribed, every officer should be able to feel
assured that his position was secure. These, my early formed and known
sentiments, need no repetition to convince officers in this county that the exercise of my *pleasure* will not be bottomed on caprice. But I hold the power
of removal as a trust, and may not decline to exercise it, when inability or
misbehaviour in office is made to appear to my satisfaction. * * I reckon
confidently on an energetic and diligent discharge of duty, a prompt and cheerful compliance with the various regulations, by which the full benefit of the
Courts may be secured to those who have occasion to use them.'"

"We will only add, Judge Gowan may be said, in a certain sense, to have
been exacting in the case of officers appointed by him, but he was just, and
that he was revered by them to the end is manifest by their final address to
him on his retirement."--"Gleanings from the Press and Public Addresses to
Judge Gowan," by a member of the Bar of Ontario, 1890.

have the force of law, but are always open to alteration by the rule-making body without resort to the Legislature.

As early as 1852 Mr. Gowan was appointed by the Crown one of five Judges authorized to frame general rules and regulations for all the Division Courts. Judge S. B. Harrison* was chairman of this Board.

In 1857, it was delegated by statute to the Judges of the Court of Queen's Bench to settle a tariff of fees for the profession and for the officers in all the Courts, and Judge Gowan was associated with them.

In 1858, new courts were established by statute, modelled something after the plan of the English Court of Probate, with all its powers touching wills and administration, and in addition the power of appointing guardians for infants who had no legal guardians, and for regulating their properties.

In the new law was a provision for the appointment of three representative Judges, who were empowered from time to time to make rules and orders for regulating procedure and practice in these Courts ; for regulating the duties of officers, the manner of appealing to the Court of Chancery from decisions ; simplifying and expediting proceedings, and fixing and regulating the fees of officers, and of attorneys and barristers practising in these Courts, and generally for carrying the provisions of the law into full and beneficial effect.

---

* Mr. Harrison was an eminent English Barrister, and author of "Harrison's Digest." He was Secretary of State in the Government under which Mr. Gowan had been appointed Judge.

In pursuance of this authority, a commission of three representative Judges were appointed by the Crown to carry out these provisions, and Chancellor Spragge, as chairman, with Judge Burns and Judge Gowan, were the three named.

The new law had been prepared for Sir John Macdonald, the Premier, by Judge Gowan, and it was left to him to draft the necessary orders, and rules, and forms, and to frame the tariff of fees. His draft was accepted by the other Judges, passed by all three, and was brought into force almost simultaneously with the new law.

The work was one of considerable difficulty, and required great care in the preparation. These rules and orders were confirmed by Act of Parliament in the following year, and both the Act itself and the rules and orders made under it have borne the strain of over thirty years actual working, and yet, it is believed, regulate these Courts. It is no little test of their excellence to have remained so long unchanged in these changing times.

The Governor had been empowered under an Act of the Legislature to appoint " a Board of five Judges " to frame general rules concerning the practice and proceedings of the Division Courts established by law in every county in the Province, and in relation to any Act respecting them " as to which doubts had arisen, or may arise, or as to which there have been, or may be, conflicting decisions in any of such Courts "; and the rules and forms, when approved, were given the same force as if included in an Act of Parliament—large and important powers these, seeing that these Courts were numerous and embraced a large share of the law business of the country.

In 1869, Judge Gowan was appointed chairman of this
Board of five Judges, and continued to hold the position
from that time up to the period of his retirement in 1883.
After his retirement from the Bench, the position being
tenable by a retired Judge, he was re-appointed chairman
of the Board by the Provincial Government and held the
position for several years after, taking much interest in the
working of the Division Courts.*

Judge Gowan's appointment in 1871, on a Commission
of Judges to enquire into the constitution and jurisdiction
of the several Courts of Law and Equity in Ontario, with
a view to the fusion of Law and Equity will be presently
further alluded to.

On two occasions the Judge was selected for extraordinary and peculiar judicial service. The first was in
1862, and in respect to a matter of much public interest.
Disputes between the Government and the Contractors
for the erection of the Parliament Buildings at Ottawa,
involving a very large amount, had been a subject of controversy for years and was unfortunately cast into the arena
of party strife. After the Hon. Mr. Brown entered the
Macdonald Government it was arranged that the matter
should be settled by arbitration ; Mr. Page, the Government Engineer, acting for the Government ; the late Mr.
Cumberland, C.E., for the contractors. It was agreed that
some Ontario Judge, both parties could agree on, should

---

* A work on these Courts was dedicated to Judge Gowan by the author
Mr. Henry O'Brien, Barrister, "in appreciation of the talents which adorn
his position, and of his exertions to forward the due and systematic administration of Justice in these Courts."

be the third. Judge Gowan was the first named, and both the Government and the contractors at once agreed to him. Of this tribunal, two only were necessary to a decision. The trial took place ; some of the ablest counsel in the country acting for the parties ; the Hon. S. Richards, Q.C., and the Hon. R. Scott, Q.C. (now Senator), for the Crown ; Mr. T. Galt, Q.C. (now Sir Thomas Galt, C.J.C.P.), for the contractors. After a protracted enquiry, the matter was brought to a close by an unanimous decision. It was said that neither party felt, as might be expected, the result to be what they desired, but it was admitted on all hands that Judge Gowan, who presided, conducted the proceedings with singular patience, judgment and ability. The award made remained unquestioned by the parties and unassailed by the public press.

The second occasion was in 1873, when very grave charges were made against Sir John Macdonald and other Cabinet Ministers, charges not only bearing upon their conduct as Cabinet Ministers, but touching their personal honor in connection with the Canadian Pacific Railway contract—" The Pacific Railway Scandal," as it was called. The matter was brought up in Parliament and a committee appointed, but owing to legal difficulties no report was made when Parliament prorogued. The matter evoked profound feeling and intense party bitterness and was used, and that successfully in the end to overthrow the Macdonald Government.

After the prorogation of Parliament, **Lord Dufferin**, the Governor-General, under the advice of his ministers, determined to issue a Royal Commission, as he had the

right to do as the Representative of Her Majesty, if on
no other grounds, because the charge touched the honor
of members of Her Privy Council ; and a commission was
accordingly issued, reciting the charges made, and directing the commission to enquire into them and report.

The commission was directed to the Honorable C. D.
Day, formerly Solicitor-General of Lower Canada, and
then a retired Judge, as chairman ; and to Mr. A. Polette
and Mr. Gowan, both of them Judges on the Bench, the
former in Quebec, the latter in Ontario. The interference
of the Governor-General in the matter was questioned by
the opposition Press all over the country. The commission was called " a whitewashing commission," " a commission for dirty work to be done," etc., and the Governor-
General was charged with acting unconstitutionally, and
with illegal interference with the action of the Commons ;
and both he and the members of the commission were
personally assailed with great acerbity by the leading
organs of the Opposition.*

Mr. Gowan's appointment was challenged on the ground
of his being a personal friend of the Premier and as one
looking for preferment on the Bench ; a preferment, as
was subsequently known, he had before actually twice

---

* "Mr. Gowan has been for the past twenty-five years the confidential
adviser and personal friend of Sir John A. Macdonald, has prepared some of
his measures, and received such favors from his hands as could be thrown in
the way of a Judge by an Attorney-General or Minister of Justice. Judge
Gowan has already done a good deal of servile work for Sir John A. Macdonald,
but has never gained the object of his aspirations. * * Perhaps he sees this
prize within his grasp at the present moment."—"The Globe."

The commission met with a good deal of obstruction, but calmly pursued the enquiry committed to them to the close, and reported the evidence taken before them. From the commencement to the end their communications lay only with the Governor-General, for they recognized fully their position as confidential agents of the Crown, and were in close communication with Lord Dufferin during the whole enquiry.

But not to dwell on a buried subject, we will only add, that when all was done and over, Judge Gowan had the satisfaction of knowing that the representative of the Sovereign highly and fully appreciated the services he was able to perform under the commission, and one of the ablest publicists in Great Britain, the Honorable George Brodrick, now Warden of Merton, Oxford, who happened to be in Canada at the time, fully approved of the course taken by the commissioners and the manner in which they conducted the enquiry. And in the debates, which afterwards followed in the Commons, the evidence taken before the commissioners was used by both parties.

We have now considered the matter in the summary coming under the heads of I., II., and III.; that falling under fourth and fifth is now to be noticed.

The masterly compositions of Jeremy Bentham, the philosopher, and great teacher for all nations, and for ages yet to come, were probably more read and studied half a century ago than now. Mr. Gowan was familiar with his works, and as a student became a convert to nearly all Bentham's views as to law reform. In respect to codification both of the civil and criminal law, Judge Gowan entertained very strong opinions, which he endeavored to impress on public men in authority in the interests of the country. As early as 1848 he discussed Bentham and his teachings with Sir John Macdonald, especially in relation to codification in our young country, and during their long friendship of over forty years he had frequent opportunities of pressing consideration of these views upon that great man. Sir John Macdonald to some extent agreed with Mr. Gowan, and quite recognized the deficiencies in our system of jurisprudence, the imperfections in our statute law, and the jumble in the statute book of Upper Canada. But his view was that a colony should move slowly, and that it was desirable to await action in the mother land, especially in the matter of codification, if on no other ground than that of expenditure, recognizing that an undertaking of the kind could only properly be accomplished through the lengthened labors of men of competent learning and thoroughly expert. But he anxiously desired to move in the lines of law reform, and to more than keep pace with improvements from time to time enacted in England. This seems to have been the great statesman's* line of action, following English enact-

---

* Mr. Dent, in his biography of Sir John Macdonald, published in 1861—though by no means a favorable estimate as a whole—admits fully his desire for progress, his readiness to adopt reforms when the country was ripe for them. And Mr. Rattray, in his admirable work, "The Scott Abroad," fully recognized this distinguished trait in his character: "Instead of the maxim 'go ahead at all hazards,' his motto," says this writer, "is 'hasten deliberately *pari passu* with public opinion;'" and he goes on to say: "In his own governmental department he was bent upon necessary reforms. To him were due the Common Law Procedure Act, the remodelling of the County Courts, and other purely legal improvements. No Government, perhaps within living

ments in the way of revision and improvements, and not many years ago he said to Mr. Gowan : "Have I not been breaking the ground. in revision and consolidation and following improvements at home ? And if I live and am in power, codification for Canada will come in time." A review of the legislation he fostered and promoted for some forty years goes to show his desire for improvement on these lines.

Attempts at general revision of the Statutes were made,* but nothing thorough was attempted until 1856, when, at the instance of Sir John Macdonald, who was then in power, another commission issued, which made a report of progress in April, 1858.†

---

memory, placed so many valuable measures on the Statute book as this one," * * "The merit, as well as the responsibility incurred, belongs in great part to Sir John Macdonald, who was at once the head and soul of the Cabinet."

* A commission was issued in 1841, to Chief Justice Robinson, Judge Macaulay, Mr. W. H. Draper, and Mr. J. H. Cameron, requiring them to examine and report on the Statute law of Upper Canada, from 1791 to the date of the Union of Upper and Lower Canada in 1841. This was a necessary work, for, with the exception of an edition of the Statutes by James Nickalls, in 1831, nothing of the kind existed. Digests of certain subjects, and some indexes, were prepared by individuals. One of these, a general index to all the Statutes in force in Upper Canada up to 1838, had been prepared by Mr. Gowan, as already mentioned, but that was all. The commission of 1841 reported in 1843, giving a mere presentation of the public general Statutes of Upper Canada as they stood in 1841, in the order of time, but without arrangement or classification, or any attempt at consolidation. A proper and complete consolidation was what was really required, and the commission, in their report, recommended as necessary a complete revision and classification.

† This commission was directed to Sir J. B. Macaulay, Adam Wilson (afterwards Sir Adam Wilson, C.J.C.P.), D. B. Read, Q.C., and S. H.

What was required, and indeed essential, was a complete classified consolidation of the whole body of Statute law in force in Upper Canada, and in a suitable shape to be laid before Parliament for adoption and enactment, with necessary tables and schedules, specially showing how every clause had been disposed of. Sir John Macdonald who had conceived the idea of a reformed Statute book—the whole Statute law of Upper Canada revised, classified, and consolidated—and was anxious for its completion and sanction by statutory enactment in improved form, appealed to Sir James Macaulay to undertake the labor of preparing it, and put the whole in shape for enactment. Sir James consented, but soon found the task too formidable to accomplish unaided. The professional men who had previously given their services, doubtless could not, without serious prejudice to their professional business, give the necessary time to the subject, and it had never been in their power, as Sir James Macaulay expressed it, " to devote to the work that continued attention which he felt to be most desirable, if not essential, to the work in hand," and as the completed work was to rest upon his own responsibility, Sir James, under the circum-

Strong (afterwards Sir Henry Strong, Chief Justice of the Supreme Court), who made considerable progress. But in their report, the commission designated their work as in an inchoate state, and without any schedule of Acts consolidated, or anything showing how each clause had been disposed of, so that the matter was not in a condition to be laid before Parliament for action. As observed by Sir James Macaulay in his report, it was not in the power of the commission to devote to the work that combined attention most desirable, if not essential, to its successful accomplishment. Numerous changes were found essential, and many corrections necessary.

stances, requested the Government to ask Judge Gowan to aid him, "entertaining a high opinion of the qualifications and abilities of that gentleman."

The Governor accordingly requested Judge Gowan's co-operation in the important work, and His Excellency's communication was backed by a personal one from Sir John Macdonald earnestly urging Judge Gowan to act. He accepted the position and immediately proceeded to join Sir James Macaulay at Toronto, and from that time gave continuous and untiring attention to the work.

The whole matter was critically examined throughout, revised, recast, and consolidated upon the plan of an improved and systematic revision of all the Statutes. The law was brought together, rendered and expressed, as under judicial construction, so as to justify the revised consolidation being substituted for the mass of scattered and detached Statutes proposed to be repealed. Titles were given and separate chapters added, repealing the Statutes superseded, and saving existing rights. For the interpretation of terms and expressions to guide and facilitate in the construction of the consolidated law, a uniformity of style was introduced, and full schedules and tables given accounting for every Statute and every existing clause, thus enabling the work to be tested.

In January, 1859, Sir James Macaulay made his report, and appended to it was the quarto volume of some 1,100 pages, which contained the revised consolidation of the Statutes relating to Upper Canada, in form to be substituted by Parliament for the mass of Statutes scattered through the Statute books since 1792. It was a formidable work, well and skilfully done, a monument of the industry, care and ability of those who prepared it, and when it came to be tried scarcely a slip or error was found in the test of practical working as a law, for it was submitted to Parliament and accepted without debate, as containing the body of the Statute law applying exclusively to Upper Canada, Parliament superseding the old enactments.

To the value of Judge Gowan's aid and assistance in the work, Sir James Macaulay bore strong testimony in his letters to the Premier and others, as well as in a letter addressed to Judge Gowan personally. In his official report, after speaking of having solicited the assistance of Judge Gowan, and his consenting to act, he adds: "He has attended from time to time, at great personal inconvenience, and we have together gone over all the public general Statutes relating to Upper Canada, and also all that portion of the joint work of consolidation, which belongs to the Upper Canada commission, and we have incorporated the Acts of the last Session with the former text. I have found Judge Gowan animated with the most lively interest in the successful issue of a work, the importance of which he fully appreciates, and I have been greatly assisted by his able co-operation. His knowledge of the Provincial Statutes throughout, and his familiar acquaintance with the details and practical working of some of the most important, as respects their general and constant use, has enabled me to correct various inaccuracies and to adopt many material amendments. A comparison of the consolidation in its present state with the form in which it was originally reported will show the additions and alterations that have been made, including, of course, the Acts of last Session."

As already observed, this consolidation became law, and the Statute provided that the public Acts of the same Session should be incorporated therewith, and the body of the Statutes, thus consolidated, proclaimed as law. Sir James Macaulay and Judge Gowan accomplished this delicate task for Upper Canada, and the test of years has shown that that learned jurist, Sir James Macaulay, was justified in speaking thus of the work : " I feel every confidence that a good work has been achieved and a desirable basis laid for future legislation. And for the able services rendered by Judge Gowan, the Government, the Legislature, and the public, as well as myself, are indebted to him." The public general Statutes applying to both Upper and Lower Canada were consolidated at the same time. G. W. Wickstead, Esquire, Q.C., the late Law Clerk of the House of Commons, a very able jurist, taking the main and chief part in that work, as Sir James Macaulay did in the consolidation applying exclusively to Upper Canada. Both Mr. Wickstead and Sir James Macaulay officially recorded their " grateful indebtedness to Judge Gowan for most valuable advice and assistance " in advancing also this difficult and laborious work to completion.

Judge Gowan again, in 1868 and 1869, at the instance of his friend the Premier, lent willing aid in preparing the several bills submitted by Sir John Macdonald, to make the criminal laws uniform all over Canada ; acting in co-operation with two permanent civil servants, Mr. G. W. Wickstead, Q.C., who was an experienced Parliamentary draftsman, and Mr. Hewitt Bernard, Q.C., the Deputy Minister of Justice, both Mr. Gowan's personal friends. With the former he had been engaged in the consolidation of 1858 and 1859. The latter, before entering the Civil Service, had lived for years in Barrie, and practised as a barrister in Mr. Gowan's Courts.

These bills embodied a consolidation of the criminal law in force in the several Confederated Provinces of the Dominion of Canada, with valuable additions and improvements in procedure and otherwise, and all were successfully promoted by Sir John Macdonald and became law, in force all over the Dominion.*

It was a valuable and necessary recast of the criminal law, and wonderfully complete so far as it covered. The work was of great importance and difficulty, for the criminal law in all the Provinces then confederated was founded on the criminal law of England, which had been introduced at different times into each. Many alterations and improvements had been enacted by the respective Provincial Legislatures, and divergence in several particulars was found to exist. The subject of criminal law and criminal procedure was assigned by the Imperial Act, confederating the Provinces, to the Parliament of Canada, and it was, of course, essential that this branch of the law should be uniform all over the Dominion.

The Ministry, to carry these measures, had to keep in view the express desire and expectation of members representing each Province, that their several systems would

---

* They appear in the Statutes of 1869, covering nearly 300 pages—chapters 17 to 37 inclusive.

be substantially embodied in the new bills introduced and so those entrusted with the preparation of the series of Acts (extending over some three hundred pages on the Statute book of 1869), had not, therefore, in all cases a free hand, for it was not thought expedient to drop any provision of any law of the several Provinces, though some had little practical general bearing under the varied conditions in widely separated Provinces. The best possible system had to be devised, and it became necessary to make extensive alterations and to introduce new provisions suited to the country and existing conditions.

In preparing these bills a wide range was wisely taken. It may be seen that the draftsmen embodied, not merely the Provincial and Dominion legislation up to the time, but also a large number of Imperial enactments, either as they stood or altered to suit the condition of the country, and did not hesitate to take some valuable provisions from the Colony of Victoria, and a few clauses from Acts in the neighboring States; and added a number of entirely new clauses. The work, therefore, in these bills was not a mere revision and consolidation, but a recast of nearly the whole body of the criminal law, improved and adapted to the new conditions of the country, and the whole appears to have been done with reference to points solved by adjudged cases.*

---

* Mr. Gowan, with the permission of the Prime Minister, saw and conferred with the Chief Justices in Upper Canada as to new provisions in the Criminal bills, and certain suggestions they made were acted on by Sir John Macdonald, who was anxious to accept all reasonable suggestions for improvement in his bills.

No doubt it was the design of the great statesman who introduced these bills to prepare the ground to lead up to codification in Canada. For it was the vast mass of ill-arranged statutes "unconnected with each other, passed at different times, written in different styles, intended for different purposes, not cast into a serviceable shape," that presented to English jurists one of the formidable difficulties in the way of codification.

And the present Premier and Minister of Justice, Sir John Thompson, must have found the work of 1869, as well as previous consolidations carried out under Sir John Macdonald's auspices, of incalculable value in facilitating the preparation of the great measure of criminal law codification, which he was enabled lately to place on the Statute book, and which will couple his name for all time with the achievement of a great and important reform.

Judge Gowan's part in this work of 1869, in co-operation with the two permanent civil servants named had no official recognition. It was voluntarily and gratuitously rendered at the instance of the Prime Minister as on previous occasions. But some seven years after, when Sir Oliver Mowat, Premier of Ontario, determined in 1876 on the consolidation of the Statute law for that Province, Judge Gowan was appointed with other Judges on a commission issued for the purpose, and rendered zealous and efficient aid in the work.*

---

* Judge Gowan's appointment on this occasion was most favorably noticed in the lay press, while the following remarks appeared in the "Law Journal" of the day: "'We are glad to learn that His Honor Judge Gowan has been added to the Commission for consolidating the Statutes of Ontario, and is

For this important service he received the thanks of the Government of Ontario who presented him with one of the gold medals struck to commemorate the event. This was a valuable and beautiful work of art and a well deserved acknowledgment, for on this, as in other matters referred to, his was a work of love—entirely gratuitous.

Judge Gowan's voluntary service in Parliamentary drafting deserves a fuller notice than our space will allow for it, extending as it did over nearly the whole period of his judicial life.

When an earnest and willing worker sacrifices none of his time to idle society but engages himself fully in a variety of subjects, it is almost incredible the amount of work he can accomplish, a complete change of subject it is said being almost equivalent to repose. This may explain the marvellous number of subjects upon which Judge Gowan employed himself, outside his regular duties, though of a kindred character, and in keeping with them. Had this labor been compulsory he might probably have found irritations, but seeing he gave his services voluntarily and gratuitously one would incline to think he found enjoyment in work.

---

taking an active part in the revision of the work already done, and in suggestion for its future prosecution. Probably no man in Canada could be found who is more familiar with the Statute book, and his ripe judgment, and the experience gained by him when on the Commission for Consolidation of the Statutes of Old Canada, will be of the greatest benefit. We congratulate Mr. Mowat on securing his services.' Everyone who knows anything of Judge Gowan will cordially endorse our contemporary's eulogy, as being eminently well deserved. The Honorable Attorney-General has certainly made a most judicious appointment."

These services in Parliamentary drafting are tersely given in the summary already referred to, as follows :— Work and assistance in the preparation of technical matter touching Legislative improvements—work which in England is done by official draftsmen and paid experts— Mr. Gowan, at the instance of the Law Officers of the Crown and under different administrations for over thirty years was so engaged.

It will be convenient to follow the order of date as given in the outline.

Parliamentary law drafting, as correctly said by the writer in the summary, is in England done by official draftsmen and paid experts, and in Canada at the present day it is so done and has been for several years past, the Deputy Minister of Justice and those acting under him doing the work in preparing measures introduced by ministers. But neither in the old Province of Upper Canada, nor in Canada after the union of the Upper and Lower Provinces, nor yet in the Dominion after Confederation was it so done, until recently.

The Provinces were young and had to provide large sums for permanent public works, the public revenue was far from large and public officers and cabinet ministers were obliged to content themselves with small incomes, and for a long time after the Union Ministers of the Crown had multitudinous duties imposed upon them, their assistance in the way of clerks and subordinates being most limited—nothing, as of recent years, in the way of experts to aid—no Parliamentary draftsman with a competent staff as in England, to whom ministers could hand over the preparation of their measures of reform, demanding knowledge of the subject and technical ability.

In the absence of such official aid, ministers had to prepare their measures unaided, or with such outside assistance from competent persons as could be obtained gratuitously, there being no legal provision for their payment.*

It was here the special aptitude and ability of Judge Gowan for such work came into play as early as 1842.†

---

* True, the Law Clerk of the House of Commons—a most competent officer—of late years gave some assistance : but, during the sittings of Parliament, he was the man of all work, and in the case of measures brought in on responsibility of the Government they had to be considered and prepared on short notice.

† And few are aware of the high qualifications necessary for a Parliamentary draftsman. Lord Thring, better known as Sir Henry Thring, the great Parliamentary draftsman, and for years the head of that department in England, last year gave a most interesting lecture before the Kensington Ratepayers' Association, on Acts of Parliament and how they are made. He had been constantly engaged from 1853 to 1886, in drafting Acts of Parliament for ministers of all parties, and of course spoke with unrivalled authority on the subject. We give one or two quotations : "What is an Act of Parliament? Take for instance," he said, "The Local Government Act of 1888. How did that Act come into existence? It did not fall from the clouds, or come, Minerva-like, fully equipped from the brain of some Parliamentary Jupiter. * * Every word of the first clause marks an era in constitutional history. * * The Cabinet having decided to bring in, say a county council bill, the President of the Local Government board sends for the Parliamentary draftsman, a permanent civil servant, and instructs him to fill in the details of the ministerial outline and put it into the shape of a complete bill. What does this imply? In the first place, the draftsman must know the law, and, in the case of a Local Government bill, this means keeping in his head the provisions of some thirty Acts of Parliament. He must know how to draft a bill. This means that he must understand the arrangement, in a lucid form, of a most complicated subject, dealing with the local details of almost all the local authorities in England, and defining their relation to the new bodies created.

The Honorable Robert Baldwin, the Attorney-General in the Government of that day, had come to know Mr. **Gowan's** ability in this way and had formed a very favorable opinion of him, and so it happened that just about the time of his appointment Mr. Baldwin employed him in drafting a measure respecting municipal government, and afterwards during the time he was in power, Mr. Gowan lent willing aid in drafting or revising a number of measures promoted

---

Although I was safely out of the way when the Local Government bill of 1888 was in the way, I know the toil which it involved, as I prepared the Local Government bills for different ministers, none of which saw the light, except a bill brought in by Mr. Goschen in 1871, which was never fully discussed. *As the foundation for these bills, I prepared abstracts and memoranda of law which would fill a folio volume of considerable size.* Again, supposing a man to have mastered the whole of the subject matter with which he has to deal, do not imagine the expression of a series of complicated enactments is an easy task. * * Try to formulate a scheme for establishing, say a friendly society, and you will see how great is the difficulty in expressing on paper, and in a manner which cannot be misconstrued, even simple propositions, still more the intricate provisions by which the new law has to be reconciled with the old. I have purposely said this to *glorify my old office*, for I was, while I held it, one of the best abused of Her Majesty's subjects."

Such are the views of this Nestor amongst Parliamentary draftsmen. He was right in every particular, for the draft bill for any important or general change in the law represents only a small part of the draftsman's labors. He is also right in saying that during the preparation of a bill the draftsman must, of necessity, be in constant communication with the minister in charge of the measure.

The difficulties are enhanced to the friendly non-official draftsman, as formerly in Canada, who has no subordinates to aid him, even in the manual work, for the confidence reposed in him forbids his seeking outside aid of any kind. And his brief for the use of the minister he aids must, of necessity, be full and complete, for when the measures come up for debate, he may not be in the way for offering explanations or answering objections that may be urged. In Canada, he has, in fact, to do all the English official draftsman has to do and more.

by that gentleman, some of which were placed in the Statute book, notably one relating to municipal law.*

It was so also in the case of Sir William Richards when Attorney-General. What that distinguished man characterized as the "voluntary and patriotic aid Mr. Gowan was willing and able to lend public men in preparing and revising important measures of law reform," was cheerfully rendered to him, in respect to a number of measures brought into Parliament during the whole time he was Attorney-General and upon many occasions, public and private, he took occasion to acknowledge Mr. Gowan's services.†

---

* Mr. Dent, in his "Canadian Portrait Gallery," published in 1880, makes the following reference to the fact : "His skill, as a legal draftsman, was such that Mr. Baldwin, who, at the time of Judge Gowan's appointment, was Attorney-General for Upper Canada, availed himself of his services in preparing various important measures, which were afterwards submitted to Parliament. This was a remarkably high compliment for a young man of twenty-five to receive ; but there is no doubt the compliment was well merited, for the measures so prepared were models of compact statutory legislation, and gained no inconsiderable *éclat* for the Administration. The example set by Mr. Baldwin, has since been followed by other Attorneys-General, and Judge Gowan has thus made a decided mark upon our Canadian legislation and jurisprudence."

And the "Canada Law Journal," of November, 1883, uses the following language : "It is well-known that many important Acts of Parliament, and many valuable amendments of existing Statutes, have originated in his fertile brain ; and any suggestion coming from this eminent Judge, with his known experience and ripe judgment, it may well be believed, was eagerly and gladly made use of by the officers of the Crown, for the time being, and speedily these suggestions would be found reflected in the Statute book."

† The aid "freely given was as generously acknowledged," and an incident is mentioned in the brochure we have before referred to in this connection. In 1863, on Sir William Richards' first appearance, as Chief Justice of Ontario, in Mr. Gowan's judicial district, the grand jury, in their final presentment, referred to the several beneficial measures in connection with the law and its

The most cordial relations existed between Sir William Richards and Judge Gowan up to the time of the former's death, and on occasions when congratulations came pouring in on Judge Gowan, the congratulations of his friend Sir William were never wanting and were always warm and appreciative.

The Honorable John Sandfield Macdonald, Attorney-General and Premier of Ontario, was another public man who frequently sought Mr. Gowan's advice and assistance in measures relating to the Courts and civil and criminal administration. He had conceived the idea of "fusing law and equity," and his Government issued a commission to enquire into the condition of the Courts with that in view. The commission consisted of Judges, of whom Mr. Gowan was one.*

The matter was worked out with a view to a report, and a bill† drafted to give it effect; but a change of Ministry

administration, he had placed upon the Statute book. In acknowledging their address, he claimed that his measures were beneficial, and that he might fairly claim also the credit every public man deserved for advocating them in Parliament; but, with regard to them and several other important measures relating to administration, he was indebted to Judge Gowan for drafting them, and he felt called upon to state that the country was mainly indebted to Judge Gowan, with whom the suggestions had originated, and he had reason to believe that other Attorneys-General had availed themselves of the suggestions and assistance of this same indefatigable authority on important measures of law reform.

* The chairman was Sir Adam Wilson, with Mr. Chancellor Strong, now Chief Justice of the Supreme Court, Mr. Gwynne and Mr. Patterson, both afterwards Judges of the Supreme Court, and Mr. Gowan.

† The bill referred to was prepared during a vacation visit Judges Gwynne and Patterson paid Mr. Gowan at Barrie, and was the work of these three members of the commission.

occurred, and the matter was put an end to, the commission being superseded before reporting.

Mr. Macdonald was in the House of Commons and became Premier of Ontario. He was not an active law reformer, but introduced and carried some valuable measures, both in the Dominion Parliament and the Provincial Legislature, in all which he sought the assistance of Judge Gowan. His Act for the speedy trial of criminal offenders without a jury was a most important one, and far reaching in operation, quite beyond, it is thought, what Mr. Macdonald had contemplated when he introduced it. The bill introduced made no adequate provision for securing uniformity of procedure, and after it became law it was obvious that it must prove a failure unless something were done to secure uniform action by all the Local Judges empowered under the new Act. When Mr. Macdonald became aware of this fact, he invited Judge Gowan to confer with him, and approved a course of action suggested by Judge Gowan which empowered the Judge to communicate with all the Local Judges on behalf of the Government, urging them to adopt the Rules which had been prepared. And Mr. Gowan was authorized to communicate the approval of these Rules by the Attorney-General to the Local Judges, who in their turn signified the adoption of the Rules, each for his own jurisdiction.

"The County Judge's Criminal Courts" now dispose of the greater part of the criminal business of the country with speed and economy, as was the design in constituting them. The whole work of these Courts is promoted by a local Crown prosecutor—the Crown Attorney—an officer appointed under Sir John Macdonald's admirable system of Crown prosecutors, of which a word will be said later on.[*]

With that great and enlightened statesman, Sir John A. Macdonald, Judge Gowan enjoyed a warm friendship, for nearly forty years, and was in the most confidential relations with him for almost the whole time he swayed the destinies of the country, constantly working for him in the preparation of his legal reforms, frequently staying with

[*] The following extract from a brochure on the "Office and Duties of the Ontario County Judge," published in 1876, will give some idea of the nature and operation of "The County Judge's Criminal Courts," and the large amount of work they performed, even at that early date:

"A Criminal Court has recently been established in every county in Ontario—The County Judge's Criminal Court—and of this the Judge is sole Judge. It is a tribunal invested with new and most important powers, viz. : Without a jury, to hear and determine, with some few exceptions, all indictable offences—felonies and misdemeanors—known to the law, save offences punishable with death, but with a right of election to prisoners to be tried by a jury, if they so desire. A very large number of criminal cases are disposed of yearly in these Courts, thus greatly reducing the work of the higher Criminal Courts, as well as the cost of the administration of justice, and, moreover, saving time and money to both grand and petit jurors, as well as to litigants having business at these Courts.

"As the County Judge's Criminal Court is constantly in session, and indeed has power to meet even while the grand jury are in session, the accused, if not guilty, is speedily released, if guilty, prompt punishment follows the crime. No such tribunals exist in the Maritime and distant Provinces ; and the jurisdiction in the Province of Quebec is not worked out by Judges answering to the County Judges in Ontario in a Court constituted by the Provincial Legislature for the special purpose. It is believed that not less than one thousand criminal cases for indictable offences were tried, without a jury, by the County Judges of Ontario, during the eleven months past of the present year, 1876—probably more than three times the number that were tried at all the other Criminal Courts in the Province before a jury."

him at his residence at the seat of Government some time
before each session of Parliament, engaged in the preparation of measures for the improvement of the law and
its administration intended for submission at the ensuing
session.

The summary above given, of draft and technical work
done for Sir John Macdonald, is by no means exhaustive,
but refers to the more important measures drafted by
Judge Gowan, several of them his own suggestion, such as
the Crown Prosecutor system, the assimilation of the law
of Probate and Administration to the English model, and
the improvement and extension of the Local Court system.
The Common Law Procedure system had been suggested
by Chief Justice Draper, and the bill was the joint work
of that gentleman and Mr. Gowan.

To enter upon a full account of Sir John Macdonald's
law measures, or even outline them, would occupy far
more space than can be given in this Memoir. It would,
in fact, be to give the history of law reform for more than
a quarter of a century, both in United Canada and in the
Dominion. Our present concern is with the friend who
rendered the Premier willing service as a draftsman in
that branch of the great man's work. We must content
ourselves with a general enumeration,* and the testimony

* One of the bills introduced by Sir John Macdonald provided for the
appointment by the Crown in every county of a permanent resident officer,
designated "The County Crown Attorney," a barrister-at-law of a certain
standing, to aid in the local administration of justice, and to perform the duties
assigned to him. The bill assigned to him the following duties :

1. To receive and examine all informations, examinations and other papers
connected with criminal charges which magistrates and coroners were required

which Sir John Macdonald himself bore to the value of
the assistance rendered to him by his friend Judge Gowan.
A few expressive words addressed to Mr. Gowan under
date 10 July, 1890, clearly shows his estimate of that gentleman's services, "When I consider all you have done in
the way of legislation for all Canada, and especially for
Ontario, I come to the conclusion they both owe you a
large debt of gratitude. * * I, for one, can never forget
all you did for me." And this was but in keeping with
reiterated public expressions from an early date by Sir

---

to send to him, and, where necessary, to cause cases to be further investigated
and additional evidence taken. To see to the attendance of witnesses, so that
prosecutions at the Assizes and Sessions should not be delayed, or fail through
want of evidence.

2. To institute and conduct, on the part of the Crown, at the Court of
Quarter Sessions for his county, all prosecutions for felonies and misdemeanors,
in the same manner as law officers of the Crown at the Assizes, and, with one
exception, with like rights and privileges.

3. To watch the conduct of criminal cases at the Sessions, where they
presented the features more of a private injury than of a public offence ; and
he was empowered to assume wholly the conduct of any case where justice
towards the accused seemed to demand his intervention.

4. To deliver papers connected with criminal business at the Assizes to
the Crown officer in attendance, and to hold himself ready to assist in prosecutions, and, in the absence of a law officer of the Crown, to take the conduct
of the criminal business at the Assizes in his county.

5. To institute and conduct summary proceedings before magistrates for
offences touching "The public revenue, the public property, the public domain,
the public peace, the public health, and any other matter made punishable on
summary conviction before magistrates ;" and he was empowered to institute
such proceedings on a complaint in writing, *or*, *as public prosecutor*, in cases
wherein the public interests required the exercise of such office.

6. To instruct magistrates, upon request, respecting criminal charges
brought before them for preliminary investigation or adjudication.

John Macdonald. Indeed, he took every occasion to acknowledge Mr. Gowan's friendly assistance, both to his
colleagues and to the public, always speaking in warm
terms of Judge Gowan and the aid he had received from
him.

It will be in order to quote his language in 1866. When
entertained by the Law Society of Upper Canada, on Sir
John's health being proposed by the chairman, who referred
to his twenty-five years of office, the wise and well considered legislation promoted by him during that time;

---

7. To perform such other services touching the office of Crown Attorney,
and the prosecution of criminal offenders, as the Governor, by regulations in
Council, might direct.

Such were the leading features in Sir John Macdonald's bill. It was
accepted by both branches of the Legislature, almost without debate, and
became law.

It was one of the most sweeping and beneficial measures ever passed in
Canada respecting the administration of criminal law, and at once accomplished a most beneficial change in the prosecution of crime, and that without
trenching upon existing rights. Something of the kind, but not so searching
or complete, had long been urged for England by its leading jurists, but little
has as yet been accomplished in that direction.

The system has now been in operation in Canada between thirty and forty
years, and, if judged by the result, the County Crown Attorney system has
amply justified the foresight and wisdom of the great statesman by whom it
was introduced and promoted. Under it the department of Government
charged with the administration of justice was at once supplied with confidential agents, appointed by the Crown, in every county. The detection,
pursuit and punishment of criminals was no longer a matter of hap-hazard,
or left to the individual sufferer, but was confided to trained professional men,
always *en rapport* with the chief law officers of the Crown.

The Crown Attorney was, in many particulars, placed in a similar position
to the Public Prosecutor in Scotland, and the excellent system existing in that
country for centuries had evidently been kept in view when framing this
measure.

Sir John, in the course of his remarks in reply, after a tribute to the memory of the late Sir James Macaulay and in equally complimentary terms alluding to the assistance he received from Chief Justice Draper, an "able legal draftsman," paid a handsome compliment to Judge Gowan: "to whom, next to Sir James Macaulay and Chief Justice Draper," said he, "I owe a debt of gratitude for assistance of this nature;" and, referring to various enactments of the Statute book, said : "If you refer to these, you will recognize the careful and legal mind and hand of my friend

---

When Mr. Gowan visited England in 1870, Mr. Russell Gurney, Recorder of London, took occasion to consult him respecting a scheme he was considering for the appointment of a Public Prosecutor in England. A bill for the purpose was subsequently introduced by Mr. Gurney, and printed by order of the House of Commons in February, 1871.

Another measure of Sir John Macdonald's, of great importance, may also be referred to.

The law with regard to Probate and Administration was in a very crude and objectionable condition when he determined to improve it. The procedure was alike imperfect and complicated. By the bill, a perfect system of decentralization, for public convenience, was established, and a proper provision for appeals instituted. We can only give an outline of the general jurisdiction, showing the nature of the important changes made, and the general range of power conferred. A "Surrogate Court," as it was called, was established in each county—a Court of law and record, over which one Judge was to preside; a registrar and necessary officers were to be appointed ; all jurisdiction was to be exercised in the name of the Queen, and the tribunals were divested of all ecclesiastical aspect. To these Courts was given full jurisdiction in all matters relating to the granting of probates of wills, and committing of letters of administration of the goods of persons dying intestate, having estates in the country, and to hear and determine all questions and suits in relation to all matters testamentary.

The granting of probate or administration was primarily to belong to the Court of the county in which the testator or intestate had his fixed place of

Judge Gowan." As well put also by a graceful writer :
"Judge Gowan was a pioneer Judge, he is yet an erudite
lawyer, and a leading mind in all great law reforms."

Sir John Macdonald's abiding appreciation of Judge
Gowan's constant services was well brought out some
seventeen years later, in a letter from him, dated 6th
November, 1883, to Sir John Rose, Bart., at one time
acting High Commissioner for Canada, as the following
extract will show :—

"He is an old and valued friend of mine ; he has just
retired from his Judgeship after a service of some forty

---

abode; and if he resided out of the country, to the Court of any county in which
the deceased left personal property. The Judge could grant probate or administration at any time, and each Court sat four times in the year, for the disposal
of contentious business, and could cause questions of fact to be tried by a jury.
When not otherwise provided for under the Act, the practice of these Surrogate Courts, so far as the circumstances of the case would admit, were to
be according to the practice of Her Majesty's Probate Court in England, to
which, indeed, the Canadian tribunals were closely assimilated in power and
practice.

On the Surrogate Courts also were bestowed the exclusive jurisdiction and
right of appointing guardians to infants, who have no father living or any legal
guardian, to take care of their persons and charge of their estates. An appeal
lay by a simple procedure to the Court of Chancery from every decision of
these Courts ; and the whole *modus operandi* had all the benefit of decentralization, and was inexpensive and expeditious. We have already referred to the
Rules for detailed procedure under the Act, in which Mr. Gowan had part.

These two measures yet remain on the Statute book, almost in the very
terms they were introduced by Sir John Macdonald, and the fact is proof of
their excellence and completeness. The same may be said of the most of Sir
John Macdonald's legal reforms, with the exception of the Common Law
Procedure Act, regulating *civil* procedure, which, on the amalgamation of the
Courts of law and equity in Ontario, after the plan of the English Judicature
Act, was necessarily changed.

years. During his incumbency he has worked earnestly with the work of legislation and in the improvement of our laws, both civil and criminal, besides helping me while Attorney-General for Upper Canada and Minister of Justice. He has been engaged in the Consolidation of the Statutes of Canada and Ontario. In fact he has worked steadily on the improvement of our laws for years ; and he might, had he been so disposed, have gone on the Queen's Bench or Common Pleas, but he preferred his comfortable and beautiful home at Barrie and his learned leisure. It was fortunate for the country that he did so, for he has had time to prepare laws, as well as to administer them, which he could not have done had he accepted such promotion." *

What Sir John Macdonald said and wrote was not merely the expression of a public man acknowledging public and personal service rendered ; the most confidential relations existed between the two men, and that entirely unselfish in character, for Judge Gowan neither sought nor expected favors of any kind from the Minister, and had indeed declined the highest judicial preferment when offered to him, as mentioned by Sir John.

Indeed, it is evident from the tenor of the Premier's letter to Mr. Gowan in 1885, after his retirement, that even

---

* In the session of 1892, Sir John Thompson, in his speech on the criminal code, thus referred to Judge Gowan : "The attention of Parliament and the public has been directed to the grand jury question very forcibly, by a member of the other branch of Parliament—a member to whom I am sure both Houses owe a great deal of gratitude, for the pains and the care and the attention he has devoted to legislation, during many years of a useful and honorable life. I refer to Senator Gowan."

the unsought position of Senator was pressed on his acceptance by Sir John Macdonald, who says : "At last the opportunity has arrived for which I have long waited, of being able to offer you a Senatorship. * * When the appointment (if you accept it, and I earnestly hope you will) is announced it will be put upon the ground of the great benefit it will be to the public to have an experienced *juris consult* like you in the Upper House ; telegraph me 'yes or no,' and be sure to say 'yes!'"

So far with regard to the judicial and technical legal services rendered by Judge Gowan, but these by no means covered all the useful labors of his long career. Others we shall now refer to.

In the organization of the Municipal system of Ontario the Judge took a great interest, and was rightly said to have largely contributed to its practical and efficient working. "Living, himself, after his appointment in a new district—brought into daily contact with the immigrant and the old settler, forced to hold his early Division Courts in localities to which, for a time, the only means of access would be a bridle path, and the only means of locomotion a saddle-horse or one's own stout legs—he was brought face to face with the wants and peculiar requirements of settlements hewn out of the primeval forest, and the learned Judge thus acquired a practical experience which was open to few. This special knowledge, added to his well known legal attainments, and the confidence which was felt in his judgment and knowledge in high quarters, gave him the opportunity to mould much needful and practical legislation—legislation which otherwise would have been largely theoretical and of questionable value. In all such matters Judge Gowan did not confine himself solely to the limited sphere of his local judicial duties, but with pen and voice brought under public notice any notable abuse, or suggested some sensible amendment of the existing law, which would bring order out of chaos, and tend to reduce the constant friction which is an incident to all newly devised systems, no matter how carefully framed. Through such labors as his—and the labors of many others, too, who are entitled to be credited with efforts in the same direction— we have perfected a most flexible and workable system of local self-government, which is a boon to the various local communities." *

Dr. Bourinot, the learned author of "Parliamentary Procedure," in his work on "Local Government in Canada," published by the "Johns Hopkins University," quotes a letter to him from the Judge touching the progress and successful working of the municipal institutions established in the Province. We give the matter as presented by Dr. Bourinot : "The author has had permission to make the following extracts from an interesting letter received by him from the Honorable J. R. Gowan, LL.D., of Barrie, Ontario, who was for over forty years actively engaged in the Judicial office, and who, in the course of his useful career, had very much to do with perfecting the flexible system of local government which the Province now enjoys : "

"' I have been familiar with our modern municipal system since it was instituted, and, with the exception of the

---

* "Canada Law Journal," 1883.

first statute passed in 1841, had something to do with the preparation or criticism of nearly every amending Act, up to the time of Mr. John Sandfield Macdonald's administration.

"'I was rather opposed to the measure of decentralization—the establishment of township councils—which did not work at all well at first. Many of the men selected for some time thereafter had neither the education nor the experience to enable them to work advantageously under the law and as respects county councils, though the number of members was large, their proceedings were in effect shaped and directed by a very few leading men. All that is changed, and the new generation are, for the most part, trained very fairly in the work of deliberative bodies, first as school trustees, then in the town and township councils. Above all other things, our excellent school system has diffused the benefits of a sound education, and given the new men enlarged views. Without these advantages the municipal institutions of Ontario, with their large powers, and the indisposition of men of means to take part in them, would have been ere this a curse to the country. The county councils are now practically schools in which men are graduated in procedure and debate, and taught something of the art of self government. It is largely from these bodies that aspirants for the House of Commons and Legislative Assembly come. I can remember that, in my own county, some eight men of this class have, in the course of years, presented themselves for the former body, and of these five were elected ; and that nine men have been returned out of twelve candidates who offered for the

Local Legislature. I take some credit to myself for an effort from the first to inspire the body in my own county with a respect for the position. I endeavored to impress on them my views of the advantage of doing things decently and in order—especially the value of well defined rules of procedure, and the importance of a strict adherence to them, and of being governed in matters not fully defined by the usages of Parliament. Even in the matter of externals, the county council of my county has shown a proper spirit, for some forty years ago the warden assumed gown and cocked hat while in the chair—a usage kept up by all these officials ever since.

"'The result of the establishment of local government in Ontario has exceeded my most sanguine expectations. I have, on several occasions, listened to debates in the county council, conducted with considerable ability and with as much decorum as one finds in the highest deliberative bodies in the country. The county council sitting at Barrie is the largest body of the kind in Canada, numbering some sixty reeves and deputy reeves; and the proportion of fair debaters is quite up to that of any Legislature I know of. But the number is now too great: that arises from the rapid increase in the population of many municipalities. As good and, perhaps, better work might be done with half the number. The time is fast approaching when the number must be limited; but it is difficult to settle the proper basis of representation, so marked is the difference in the populations of the several townships and towns.

"'Taking it all in all, however, municipal government

in Ontario is a success ; there is nothing elsewhere equal
to our system. It has its evils ; amongst them, the mode
of assessment by officers appointed in and acting for each
locality. "Log-rolling" is not unusual when the assessment of the county comes to be equalized. But on the
whole, I repeat, the system has turned out well, on account
of the diffusion of education and the general distribution
of property, not to speak of the race of British blood who
have developed it.

"'These causes, together with annual elections, have
been the great safeguards for the due execution of the
large powers conferred on the municipal bodies.'"

" To the foregoing testimony, I may add the following
passage from an answer, by the same high authority, to
an address presented to him not long since, by the council
of the county of Simcoe, where the municipal system has
been worked out in its completest form : "

"'We can now fairly claim that we possess the most
perfect system of municipal government enjoyed by any
country, and have proved that an intelligent and educated
people may be safely entrusted with the management of
important matters demanding local administration—matters that would but retard and embarrass the proceedings
of the higher legislative bodies, if indeed they were *there*
able to secure the attention they deserved. In many respects our county stands foremost, and, having watched
its progress from the primitive condition of a 'new settlement,' I am filled with admiration of the patient industry
and intelligent energy that have accomplished so much in
a period of forty-one years. You know that at first we

had barely passable roadways through the 'woods'; that farming operations were conducted in a very imperfect way ; that commerce and manufactures were scarcely in the bud ; that the few schools which existed were imperfectly served and ill-regulated ; while the municipal system was a recent creation, and, moreover, that ready submission to the law of the land was *not* universal. Many of you will remember the time when this state of things prevailed, and will know what a contrast presents itself as you now look around you—the whole country accessible by excellent roads and, more than that, netted all over with railways ; agriculture, in its various aspects, carried on intelligently by an educated farming community ; free public schools, with efficient teachers, under a uniform system, within easy access of all ; the laws everywhere respected and cheerfully obeyed ; and last, though not least, our municipal system, permeating every part with its healthy influences—yes, when you look around you, you cannot help feeling that ours is a happy and honorable position, and must bless God every day that your lot is cast in a free country, where there is work for all and bread for all ; where honest labor meets its appropriate reward, and where any deserving man in the community may aspire to the highest place and the largest power for serving his country.'"

The municipal councils in his district were very sensible of Mr. Gowan's constant aid, and passed, on many occasions, resolutions of thanks to him for his assistance. Some of these addresses we shall have occasion to refer to hereafter.

In the cause of Education, Mr. Gowan has always been an earnest and conspicuous worker, in connection with the public school system, as well as with the institutions for higher education. He was chairman of "The Board of Public Instruction," in the district, from 1844 to 1871. This body, for some thirty years, performed the duty of examiners for teachers of all grades in the public schools, and, to a certain extent, that of visitors and inspectors. An alteration in the system in 1871, transferred these duties to salaried inspectors and officers working directly under the Education Department, at the seat of Government. But for nearly thirty years Mr. Gowan faithfully fulfilled the duties of chairman of the board, with advantage to the public and acceptably to the members of the board—ministers of the various religious denominations.

In 1843, a grammar school, with state endowment, was established in Barrie, and a chairman and trustees appointed by the Government, empowered to select masters and superintend the management of the institution. Judge Gowan was appointed a trustee in 1843, and afterwards, on the death of the first chairman, the Rev. S. B. Ardagh, the rector of the place, was appointed in his stead chairman of the Barrie Collegiate Institute, to which rank the school had attained. This he held up to 1892, when he resigned, after forty-nine years' service in connection with the institution.*

---

* On the 19th December, 1892, when Senator Gowan resigned the position as Chairman of the Collegiate Institute Board, the board passed the following resolution, which was published in the papers of the day :

" In accepting the resignation of Senator Gowan of his position as Chair-

The appointments of chairman and trustees were at first, and for some years, made by the Crown ; but afterwards the power of appointing was transferred to the representatives of the people in their county councils, the tenure being for three years ; but Mr. Gowan's appointment was invariably renewed at the expiration of every term. The chairman was elected annually by the board.

The Barrie institution is, perhaps, the only body of the kind in Canada in which a complete feeling of harmony and action prevailed for half a century.*

man of the Board of the Barrie Collegiate Institute, the board desires to place on record the high sense which it entertains of the services rendered to the institute, and to the educational interests of the community, by Senator Gowan, during his long connection with the board. Senator Gowan has occupied a position on the board for the long period of forty-nine years, having entered on his duties as trustee in the year 1843. During twenty-one years of that time he has occupied the position of chairman, having been appointed to that office in the year 1871. Throughout the whole of this period his services have been rendered with unfailing fidelity and punctuality, while his warm sympathy with the work of the institute has contributed much to the success of the school, and to the comfort of the staff. His thorough knowledge of the law, and his interest in, and acquaintance with the history of educational work in all its relations, were at all times of the highest use to his colleagues, and to the institution of which he and they had the oversight and direction. His genial and judicious conduct in the chair, carried the board through the frequent perplexities of its work without friction, and with the best results for the duties entrusted to it. The board has pleasure in placing this inadequate tribute to Senator Gowan's work on its records, and, at the same time, expresses its satisfaction that, though retiring from the position of chairman, he has consented in the meantime to continue to occupy the position of trustee."

* It is a remarkable fact that, in forty-nine years, this board had only two chairmen—the Reverend S. B. Ardagh and Judge Gowan—and on the latter's retirement, his brother-in-law and successor in the office of Senior Judge, Mr

In connection with education, it must be mentioned that to Judge Gowan the profession in this Province owed the establishment, in 1855, of their first legal periodical, "The Upper Canada Law Journal," which has continued its prosperous career to the present time.*

To this publication he was, for many years, the main and almost the only contributor of original matter, and afterwards largely aided with material support to keep the publication abreast of the requirements of the day, and

---

J. A. Ardagh, was elected chairman. The institution itself has always been conspicuous for the high standing of its masters, the excellence and thoroughness of its work, and is one of the most popular seats of learning in the Province. Many men who have attained eminence in the professions, as well as in public life, hail from this school.

* The profession had no organ in the Province, and those outside of Toronto were at a great disadvantage in respect to judgments in Chambers, which, if they reached them at all, came in a very imperfect form; and, moreover, the decisions of the local Judges were not in any reports, and the value of many of them was confined to a single district. There were several hundred local Courts, with two or more officers for each who naturally desired to know what was doing in other Courts. And so with regard to the numerous municipal bodies throughout the country, there was no medium of communication between them, no means of learning anything of their doings, unless a case came up in appeal to the Courts at Toronto. There was small prospect, under such a condition, for securing uniformity of practice and procedure.

Judge Gowan thought that if a legal journal could be established, at first mainly directing its efforts to local administration of every kind, much good might be accomplished, and that such a publication would, in the end, lead to something better. He was essentially a law reformer, and, seeing difficulties in reaching the public through an impartial publication that he could properly communicate with—a non-political journal—he opened a suggestion for the establishment of such a law publication to the Honorable James Patton, who was then the proprietor of a political journal published in Barrie. After a conference between them, it was agreed to publish a monthly law journal, for which Mr. Gowan was to supply all the leading articles, Mr. Patton taking

this with a single eye to legal reform and improvement, and without seeking or obtaining any pecuniary advantage to himself. It is not for the writer, in this sketch, to speak of the benefits of such a publication, but one fact may be mentioned—that many improvements in the law, advocated in the early years of the " Law Journal," are now to be found on the Statute book. With the same unselfish feeling, Judge Gowan was ever ready to aid those who entered the field of legal literature.

---

charge of all the details and printing at his newspaper office. The Judge's name was not to appear, but everything in the paper was to be submitted for his approval. He advanced the money for suitable type, etc., and agreed to indemnify against any loss in publication ; but any profit in the concern was to belong to Mr. Patton, and he was to hold himself personally liable for necessary outlay, having the whole pecuniary advantage from the publication.

Mr. Patton secured the assistance of his partner, Mr. Hewitt Bernard, afterwards Deputy Minister of Justice, and for some years this arrangement continued until Mr. Patton left the district. The Judge, during the whole of that time, wrote the leading articles, and contributed more than two-thirds of the remaining original matter. Such plant as there was, and all right in the publication, belonged to Judge Gowan, and when Mr. Patton and Mr. Bernard gave up, the publication was handed over by Mr. Gowan to Mr. Richard Bernard, Barrister, on similar conditions, and afterwards, when the place of publication was changed to Toronto, Mr. Gowan arranged for its conduct by Mr. W. D. Ardagh and Mr. R. A. Harrison, Barristers. The former of these gentlemen became a Judge in Manitoba, the latter Chief Justice in Ontario. Finally the publication fell into the hands of Mr. Henry O'Brien, Barrister, who was a writer in the journal, and he still continues to publish it. The journal has been in existence now for some thirty-five years, and during the whole of that time Mr. Gowan neither sought nor obtained any profit from the publication or the moneys he invested in the undertaking. After Mr. Harrison became connected with the Law Journal, Mr. Gowan wrote only occasionally for it, but in its early years he used it largely in advocating many law reforms, several of which were adopted by the Legislature and became law. Although it was a sort of open secret that Mr. Gowan really controlled the journal, his n me never appeared upon it, as editor or conductor.

In this connection may also be mentioned the ever ready aid Mr. Gowan was willing to give to those anxious and able to pay something of the debt that every man owes to the profession to which he belongs.

Mr. Gowan had been collecting material with a view to a work on municipal law ; all this he placed at the disposal of the late Chief Justice Harrison, when he found that that gentleman had undertaken such a work, and read and revised upon every page of the "Common Law Procedure Act" and "Municipal Manual," as Mr. Harrison, in his preface and otherwise, most gracefully acknowledged. And so with Mr. O'Brien, in his well-known "Manual on Division Court Law ;" and Mr. Boys, now a Junior Judge in Mr. Gowan's old Judicial district, in his excellent work on "Coroners,"—the Judge showed the same desire to aid young authors. Both these gentlemen expressed their appreciation and respect by dedicating their works to him.*

Moreover, during the whole time Mr. Gowan sat on the Bench, he took occasion, in his addresses to grand jurors, to deal in an instructive way, critical and suggestive, not merely with questions of jurisprudence, but with a variety of kindred topics of general interest.

---

* A new and greatly enlarged and improved edition of Judge Boys' work on Coroners has just been issued, also dedicated to Senator Gowan, in the following terms : To the Honorable James Robert Gowan, C.M.G., D.C.L., Senator of the Dominion of Canada, to whom, in 1864, was dedicated the first edition of this work, I now, after the lapse of twenty-nine years, dedicate this third edition, the last, in all probability, that will be published in acknowledgment of a long, uninterrupted and valued friendship, during which I have been the recipient at his hands of many kindnesses, and among which was the original suggestion to me of preparing a work on the office of Coroners.

His addresses were always well considered and oppor-
tune. The review of recent legislative enactments was
frequently a prominent feature in these addresses, and, as
remarked by "Bystander" and other public writers: "His
utterances always command respect." "His opinions are
of great weight, and will doubtless have influence in the
discussion of the subject in Parliament." "Judge Gowan
always makes a number of sensible and very timely remarks." "Some of the Judge's addresses were elaborate
compositions. One is now before the writer, in the form
of a re-publication, with notes by the late Honorable
James Patton, Q.C., under the caption of "The Canadian
Constable's Assistant." It is really a treatise on the
numerous and important duties of peace officers—a com-
pendium of the law on the subject. And so with regard
to others of his many addresses on the grand jury system,
quoted by Mr. Kane in his admirable little work on the
subject.

We have given a brief notice of the Judicial labors of a
pioneer Judge in Canada, and referred to some important
work in the public interest in which he was engaged.
Actively employed in the Judicial office for nearly forty-
one years, a longer service than that of any other Judge
in Canada, it is not a matter of surprise that much interest
should be felt in a career, without parallel for duration in
any colony of the Empire, marked as it was throughout,
and to the very close, by a vigorous discharge of every
duty, as well as by varied and important services, outside
the duties proper of the office he held. His official life
was one of uniform and extended usefulness. As was

truly said of Judge Gowan, he was no ordinary man, and his retirement from office was no ordinary event, and it was but natural to suppose he would carry with him into his well-earned retirement the approving testimony of those who recognize the value of courage, rectitude and ability in the discharge of important public functions.

Judge Gowan unexpectedly retired from the judicial office in October, 1883; and from the abundant expression through the public press, from the profession, and from public bodies, it will be our pleasant task to select some tributes to his well spent forty-one years in the service of the Crown. It is pleasant to his friends and admirers to know that, notwithstanding his abundant labors, Mr. Gowan is still active in mind and body. He had refused the highest preferment in the profession; if he had chosen, his age did not preclude the idea of continued judicial usefulness, and every one thought he was determined "to die in harness." He had no doubt undergone trying hardships in the early settlement of the new district to which he was appointed, and to which a man with a less elastic constitution would have succumbed.* But though they

---

* Living himself, after his appointment; in a new district, the only means of locomotion was a saddle horse or one's own stout legs, for the position of a Judge " was attended in those days with a good many inconveniences which have disappeared with advancing civilization. The roads were in such a condition that he was generally compelled to make his circuits on horseback. Judge Gowan's district was the largest in the Province, and stretched over a wide tract of country, the greater part of which was but sparsely settled. He was frequently compelled to ride from sixty to seventy miles a day, and to dispose of five or six hundred cases at a single session. One of the newspapers published in the county of Simcoe gave an account, several years ago, of some

were not without producing their effect upon his health, they were not, probably, the operating cause of his retirement. He, himself, says in his address to the Bar: "Let me say one word as to my retirement. As you are aware, this is the largest judicial district in the Province, having a population, not very long since, equal to that of Manitoba and British Columbia together. The duties are very onerous, requiring the services of at least two more active men to perform properly with the promptitude demanded in the various duties made incident to the Judge's office, and I felt the time had come when, in justice to the public and my brother Judges, I should make way for a younger

---

of his early exploits, from which account it appears that he was often literally compelled to take his life in his hands in the course of his official peregrinations. It describes how, on one occasion, he was compelled to ride from Barrie to Collingwood when the forest was on fire. The heat and smoke were sufficiently trying, but he had also to encounter serious peril from the blazing trees which were falling all around him. On another occasion, while attempting to cross a river during high water, his horse was caught by the flood and carried down stream at such a rate that he might well have given himself up for lost. He saved himself by grasping his horse's tail, and thereby keeping his head above water until he came to a spot where he could find foothold, and so made the best of his way, more than half drowned, to the shore. On still another occasion, crossing the ice from one point on Lake Huron to another, for the ice extended several miles out into the lake, the whole field of ice moved bodily out from the land, and he barely escaped, his horse having to plunge through the water between the ice field and the shore."—"Law Journal" and "Canadian Portrait Gallery." "Mr. Gowan," says the able and accomplished author of "The Irishman in Canada," "is one of the most venerable and learned figures on the Bench. When, in 1842, Mr. Baldwin made him Judge of the district of Simcoe he was the youngest Judge of the Province. Many a time in those days he had to ride seventy miles a day to meet his Court engagements, and his adventures by flood and field would make a little volume: yet he was scarcely ever absent from his duties."

man. My age and uncertain health demanded more repose than I could properly ask or take, and so I sought retirement, and after forty-one years of hard work it cannot be said that my appeal to be relieved was in any sense premature. Indeed, I have the satisfaction of knowing that His Excellency the Governor-General appreciates, as he is pleased to communicate, my 'faithful, efficient and impartial conduct during my long term of judicial service.'"

The Judge could, probably, have gone on without remark or complaint, doing such work as uncertain health permitted; but he evidently felt that it was not consistent with a proper sense of duty to retain office when unable to give the full measure of service he had been accustomed to perform. Retirement meant a diminished income; but he had evidently made up his mind as to what was right to do, and did it without hesitation; not even, we believe, advising with anyone on the subject. Certain it is, as already mentioned, it took the public, the Bar, and even his own intimate friends by surprise, for, up to the day it was announced, he had held the Courts, as well as discharged the duties of Chambers, with all his accustomed energy and assiduity. The first public announcement was in the early part of October, 1883, and a few extracts from the public journals may serve to show the feeling that prevailed. "As we go to press," said the Law Journal, "we notice the retirement of His Honor James Robert Gowan. * * Those only, and the circle of these is no limited one, who know of his learning, his large and ripened experience, and his great service to the country in numberless ways, can measure the loss this will be to the Bench, of which he was *facile princeps.* * * Judge Gowan occupies as strong a position in the hearts of his friends and acquaintances, from his high personal character, as from his judicial excellence. A kind thoughtfulness for others, and a benevolent disposition, endeared him to the community in which he has heretofore passed his long and useful life. Spotless purity, entire freedom from undue influence, and an earnest desire to do justice, have characterized him as a Judge. Great force of character, combined with cordiality and courtesy of demeanour, and a high consideration for the performance of his duties, have distinguished him as a citizen. * * He takes with him into his well-earned retirement, the best wishes of a large circle of friends and admirers for his future health and happiness ; and we trust that, in some way or another, the country may still have the benefit of his ripe experience. His career is a brilliant example to those who occupy similar positions of trust and dignity, to emulate which will be a duty, and to equal which will indeed be difficult."

In the public press it was generally recognized that, after so long a service, he naturally desired to withdraw from active judicial work. "The esteem for Judge Gowan," said one paper, " extends far beyond official circles : he is well-known in spheres of Christian philanthropy, and his efforts in doing good have, in many cases, led to happy results."

" He has been longer on the Bench than any other Judge in the Dominion, and has made a very honorable record.

His services have been recognized by magistrates, lawyers, and the public generally ; and he enjoys the respect and esteem, not only of his brother Judges and the members of the Government, but of all with whom his duties have brought him in contact. We know of no occupant of the Bench who, by long service and the faithful discharge of his duties, has so richly earned retirement as has Judge Gowan."

" Whilst we, in common with the community at large, cannot but regret that Judge Gowan has left the Bench, of which he was so distinguished an ornament, we can easily understand that he wished to divest himself of the ermine whilst his mental faculties were undoubtedly unimpaired and in more than youthful vigor, because tempered by years and enlarged and varied experience, and cultivated, by not merely legal lore, but by extensive literary reading and study, which it is to be hoped, now that he is untrammelled by judicial fetters, the country may at no distant day reap the benefit of, in some form or other."

We might multiply quotations in this connection, for the subject was noticed very generally by the public press, and all, without exception, gave expression to regret, and spoke in eulogistic terms of Judge Gowan's varied services during his long career. It is believed they spoke the mind of every thinking man in the community, and we are borne out in this by the language of the presentment by the grand jury for the county in which he resided so long, at the Court next after the Judge's resignation :

" This being the first grand jury that has met since the

retirement of Judge Gowan, we cannot allow the opportunity to pass, without expressing our high sense of the long and faithful service he has rendered in this county. * * We take peculiar pleasure, being in a sense representatives of the people of this county, in placing on record our high sense of the great esteem and respect in which Judge Gowan has always been held by the residents of this county, and in doing this we know that we are voicing the unanimous sentiments of all. Judge Gowan has many happy causes for gratification in looking over his long judicial course, and we think it will not be least among them to know, that he always carries with him the goodwill and highest esteem of the people with whom he has been so long identified."

To find such unanimity of expression touching any public man is rare, and especially one who, in the position of a pioneer Judge, must have many a time crossed influential interests ; but his fearless honesty was only equalled by the kindly and judicious way in which many an unpleasant duty was performed. His field of usefulness was large, and he was restless in his efforts to serve, and, as a consequence, the careers of few public men have been marked by such constant and varied appreciation. The municipal councils all over that large district, on many occasions, in resolutions and addresses, thankfully acknowledged his services in connection with municipal institutions. The officers of his Courts rendered cheerful service, grateful for his ready instruction and desire to please.

He was revered and loved by the profession—many of

his Bar, at the time he retired, he had known from their childhood—and they were justly proud of his well-deserved fame. It might well be supposed that his retirement would elicit expression from these quarters ; but, before speaking of what was then done, we go back to the period in 1868, when Judge Gowan had completed a quarter of a century on the Bench. To mark the occasion, he was presented by the Bar with a life-sized portrait of himself, in his robes. The portrait was accompanied by an enthusiastic address, expressive of the respect and esteem in which he was held by the donors. We extract a couple of paragraphs: "We feel that to your wise counsels and examples are mainly due the existence of a Bar in this county, which will compare favorably with any in the Dominion, and that this result has been obtained without, in the smallest degree, fostering it at the expense of the public interest. * * We believe that to your firm and dignified administration of the laws is mainly to be attributed the comparative freedom from crime which, we rejoice to know, distinguishes the county of Simcoe, and the respect for law and order which pervades all classes of our community.

"The profession have long felt that some public recognition of your extended and valuable services on the Bench, and your kindly spirit towards themselves, was due to you, and we now beg your acceptance, at our hands, of this life-sized painting of yourself, in your official chair and robes, as a mark of the respect and esteem in which you are held by us ; and while making it, as we do, your own private property, we ask the favor, that it may for a time be permitted to hang in the Court-room, so that all may have an opportunity of seeing it, and learning that the profession have paid tribute to your worth." *

The occasion also was commemorated by an address from the municipal council of the district, expressive of their "lively appreciation of his long judicial service," and assuring him "that the same sentiments of esteem and high respect that animated the council towards him were equally shared by the public at large."

On these graceful acts the public press commented in terms of approval, and it must have been gratifying, as it was encouraging, for him to feel that he retained the regard and respect of the profession, and the representatives of the people, to the very close of his career on the Bench.

We have already said that the announcement of Judge Gowan's retirement from the Bench, in 1883, took every-one by surprise ; but it had scarcely become public when the Bar, the officials of the Courts, and the county officers took steps to give expression to their feelings. At a meeting of the Bar, called on the occasion, it was resolved to present the Judge with a suitable address and a testimonial, in the form of a piece of plate. The officers of the Courts determined to do likewise, as did the county officials.

These several addresses—each in itself a fine specimen of the illuminating art—were enclosed in beautifully enriched frames, and were all three presented to the Judge

* The address was signed by every member of the Bar and every practitioner in the district. Many of them have since passed away, and some who have moved to the seat of the Courts at Toronto, as Mr. D'Alton McCarthy and Mr. William Lount, still retain their business connection with and are represented in legal firms in Barrie.

on the same occasion, the very day before he left home, for a visit to England. The public journals fully reported the proceedings, and we give a condensed account from the several reports.

The presentations were made in the large Council Chamber, at Barrie, in the afternoon of the 15th day of October, 1883. A large assembly of ladies and gentlemen were present to witness the ceremony, besides those who took part in it. "The sombre spectacle of a group of gowned barristers would, at any other time, have compelled the idea of tiresome, intricate and angry argument; but, on the present occasion, peace, good-will and respect were enshrined in the hearts of the many participants in the demonstration. In a word, the occasion was the formal expression of farewell on the part of the barristers, solicitors, officials, and Division Court officers of the county, to His Honor Judge Gowan, on his retirement from judicial life and temporary departure from Canada. It was a ceremony fraught with much food for reflection. It was a tribute to a life of many years of judicial energy and perseverance, at a time when the institutions of civilization in this part of Canada were only inceptive. It was more than that—it was the crystallized recognition of scholarly distinction in the judiciary of the Dominion of Canada No one acquainted with the history of the subject of these words can accuse us of fulsomeness, in saying that the natural and acquired ability of Judge Gowan has left an indelible impression on the judicial history of Canada; and that his name as a jurist will continue to hold an important place in the annals of this country."

At about three o'clock p.m., His Honor, accompanied by Wm. Lount, Esq., Q.C., entered the Chamber, and was ushered to a seat immediately in front of the Bench, the Bar greeting his entrance by rising. The crier of the Courts commanded "silence," and Mr. Lount proceeded to read the following address, the members of the Bar standing :

His Honor James R. Gowan, etc., etc.,—

We, the practising barristers and solicitors of the Judicial District of Simcoe, cannot allow the occasion of your retirement from the judicial Bench to pass without testifying, however inadequately, the high esteem in which we hold you, and our regret that the relations so long existing between us, are about to be severed.

The benefits derived by this county during the last forty-one years* from your high attainments and administrative ability, have been incalculable. Courts have been organized ; the legal business has been conducted with precision and decorum ; and the judgments you have

---

* Mr. Gowan had the honor of being personally known to the late Lord Cairns, and visited at "Lindesfarne" in the winter of 1884. In a letter from that great and good man to a near relative of Mr. Gowan, dated Lindesfarne, 18th April, 1884, he thus speaks of the Judge's long services :

"I read the very graceful address presented to Judge Gowan on his retirement from the Bench, and his most interesting answer. The term of his occupation of the Bench is most remarkable. I doubt if there has been its equal in this country, and I rejoice and wonder at it the more when I see his eye undimmed, his natural force unabated. I will have the opportunity of calling to see the testimonial in London."

The testimonial referred to was the piece of plate presented to Mr. Gowan by the Bar.

given in the vast number of cases that have come before you, have been luminous, dignified and impartial. Nor can we forget that some of the most important enactments on our Statute book owe their development and moulding into shape to the sagacious advice you were at all times willing to afford when called on by the rulers of the State.

And not to this place alone have your services been beneficial, for your system of organization, and the example of your Courts, have spread beyond our borders, and have had marked influence in every county of the Province. But space will not permit us to enlarge on this, otherwise we should be led into a general reference to the affairs of the Province, and possibly of the whole Dominion, so great has been the influence of your abilities and industry in various directions, during your term of office.

To us you have ever been courteous, considerate and kind ; to your discouragement of all that is unworthy, by your inspiring sense of honor, we attribute the high standing we have attained, and we feel assured that the tradition of your career will be long remembered, not only by the generation now living, but by those who may come after us.

We accordingly contemplate, with affectionate concern, the withdrawal from us of one to whom we owe so much.

We trust, however, that your intended sojourn in a more genial climate will produce every good result, and that, under the care of an all-disposing God, your return to us may be the commencement of a new era in your life, and you may be enabled to pursue it with continued usefulness.

That you may be sometimes reminded of the cordial relations that existed for so many years between yourself and the Bar of the county of Simcoe, we desire to present you with a piece of plate, which we know you will value, not for its intrinsic worth, but for the feelings that prompted the gift.

The address was handed by Mr. Lount to Judge Gowan, who read the following reply :

Mr. Lount and Gentlemen,—

I thank you with all my heart for the kind address with which you have honored me. I wish I could feel that I fully deserved all you say. Ever sensible of my many deficiencies, I tried to make up for them by a laborious assiduity and exactitude in fulfilling every known duty, to the utmost of my ability. It is the only merit I can claim, and I am by no means sure I could have done much, had I been without the stimulus which a learned and energetic Bar always gives to the Bench. And now, in retiring from the accustomed scene of my labors, and severing the relations that have connected us for so many years, the sadness, to me, is soothed by the regrets you express; and the approving testimony you bear to my humble services is the best award any public servant could desire.

When I recall the state of things as they were when I first set foot here, and the wonderful improvements that have, since 1843, been effected in our legal, municipal, and educational systems, the increased facilities for travelling, and the marvellous progress and prosperity of the country at large, there is opened to me a wide and pleasant field for observation, upon which I should like to dwell, but it is not possible to do so at present. This I may say, however: in no particular is progress so marked as in the growth of the Bar here and elsewhere, in numbers, in influence and trained knowledge.

The rapid flight of time is brought before me, when I remember that, of the present large Bar, several of the seniors were school boys when I was appointed to the judicial office, and several others were born since my first Court was held in the district. It has been my great good fortune to be surrounded and aided in the discharge of my official duties by those whom I have known from their childhood, and never, in a single instance, has anything disturbed the pleasant relations between the Bench and the Bar in this judicial district. You can understand, then, how warmly I reciprocate all you can possibly feel towards me. I well know that the industry and ability of the Bar has smoothed many a difficulty for me in the way of judicial investigations, and it is exceedingly gratifying to me to recall the high professional tone which always prevailed, and could always be safely confided in, being grounded on convictions of duty, and a nice sense of honor —securing a liberality in practice beneficial to clients, and speeding the disposal of matters really in dispute between litigants. I am proud to know that this Bar is conspicuous in the Province for the ability of its members, the number who have attained high position in their own peculiar field, as well as in public life, who have ably served the public in the Courts and elsewhere, with all the honesty, zeal and courage which have secured for our honorable

profession its high standing amongst an educated and
most intelligent people, very tenacious of their rights—
such is the simple fact; and if, indeed, I have in any degree
impressed upon the profession my views of their honorable
and responsible duties, I feel thankful indeed. I may
repeat what I said on an occasion similar to the present,
that I felt it was right that I should endeavor to discharge
every duty, faithfully and fearlessly, to create confidence
in and to secure to suitors the full benefit of the several
Courts over which I presided, and to impress the public
with the feeling of respect never withheld from a Court of
Justice, however limited its sphere, where order and decorum obtain ; that from the first I felt that this could best
be done with the aid of an educated and honorable Bar,
who could feel with me that we were all ministers of justice—all equally striving for the same great end. What I
said fifteen years ago I can emphatically repeat, that from
the profession in this county I have always received the
greatest aid in the discharge of my judicial duties, and it
is to your cordial co-operation and support I am indebted
for a measure of success that, unassisted and unsupported,
I could scarcely have obtained. In gladly according to
the Bar every privilege they could fairly claim, in fostering
a right feeling in their intercourse with each other, in pub-
licly combating prejudices against them, I have ever felt
I was strictly within the line of duty ; but I think you will
acquit me of the weakness which fails to look for the
inherent merits of a case in admiration for the skill and
zeal of counsel.

The kind consideration you have always shown me I

have every confidence you will extend to my successors. It is a consolation to me to know that my learned brother Judge Ardagh takes my place; educated in the country, and with an experience of some ten years on the Bench, the profession and the public will not lose by the change. You all know Mr. Boys, who will be the Junior Judge, and his very honorable position at the Bar. With two such worthy men on the Bench of this judicial district, both in the prime of life, the profession and the public, I repeat, will gain by my retirement.

Though giving up active duty, I shall still consider myself, in a sense, with harness on my back, being empowered still to take occasional duty ; and I may mention that the Government of Ontario continues me in the position of Chairman of the Board of Judges.

Let me say one word as to my retirement : As you are aware, this is the largest judicial district in the Province, having a population, not very long since, equal to that of Manitoba and British Columbia together. The duties are very onerous, requiring the services of at least two active men to perform properly with the promptitude demanded in the various duties made incident to the Judge's office : and I felt the time had come when, in justice to the public and my brother Judges, I should make way for a younger man. My age and uncertain health demanded more repose than I could properly ask or take, and so I sought retirement, and, after forty-one years of hard work, it cannot be said that my appeal to be relieved was in any sense premature. Indeed, I have the satisfaction of knowing that His Excellency appreciates, as he is pleased to communicate, my "faithful, efficient and impartial conduct during my long term of judicial service." You are good enough to refer to other work I have been engaged in— I did try to be of some use outside my official engagements, when employed in matters of public interest and concern. It was, I felt, only my duty to render such willing aid as was required of me, by those who were anxious to promote all that was good and safe in the improvement of the law and its administration, and who were in the high position which enabled them to give effect to their desires. And should I return, as I trust I shall, with restored health, I hope to find some opening for usefulness, for I feel that I am not without a residuum of energy, and I could not well live an idle life.

I would fain say more, and with all the warmth that words can convey, but you will know how much I am occupied, as I leave for England to-morrow, and how disturbing are necessary preparations, and will excuse my imperfect expression of thanks. I should, indeed, be insensate if I were not touched deeply by your kindness. I may well feel honored by this last mark of your regard, by the more than kind words you have addressed to me. I am deeply grateful—but not content with words, you have thought it right to order a piece of plate to be presented to me ; I can but accept your gift at such time as you think proper to give it. I did not need it to deepen the impression your generous testimony has made upon me. Whatever it may be, I shall prize it as my most valued possession, more to me than any other honor that could be conferred, for you use it to set the seal, as it were,

to what you in your spontaneous kindness have said. It
is not the only token I have had from the profession of
their regard, and I should feel humbled to the very dust
if I had not aspired from the first to accomplish some of
the good, that in your partial judgment you couple with
my poor efforts.

I would thank you, once again, for the unbroken attention, respect and kindness of years, and my earnest prayer
is, that God may bestow upon you, and those dear to you,
His richest blessings here, and an eternal life beyond.

I bid you an affectionate farewell.

After a brief interval, the High Sheriff, at the head of
the county officials, approached to where His Honor was
standing, surrounded by the Bar, and read the following
address :

His Honor James R. Gowan, etc., etc.,—

We, the undersigned officials of the county of Simcoe,
having heard, with sincere regret, that your Honor has
resigned your judicial office, a position that you have so
ably and honorably filled for upwards of forty-one years,
to the entire satisfaction of all classes of the community,
cannot allow your Honor to withdraw from your official
position without an expression of unfeigned sorrow at the
severance from us of a gentleman with whom we have
been so long officially connected, and whose wise counsels
were always beneficial to us in the discharge of our multi-
farious and often perplexing duties.

We cannot but remember the early days, when your
official duties required you to travel what was then a

wilderness, but what has since been converted into peaceful homesteads, peopled by a law-loving and law-abiding community, and we are not saying too much when we say that the law and order for which this county is noted is, in a great measure, attributable to your Honor's wise and firm but gentle administration of justice.

We trust that yourself and Mrs. Gowan may have a pleasant tour, and return before long to the county in which so many of your best years have been passed.

We feel satisfied, notwithstanding your retirement from the Bench, that your matured knowledge will not be lost to the country, but that, in some shape, the community will yet receive the benefit of the vast amount of experience that you have acquired during so long and active a public life.

To this address, the Judge's reply was as follows :

Mr. Sheriff and Gentlemen,—

While it is a source of deep and sincere gratification to me to receive from you an address conveying such kindly expressions of appreciation and regard, I cannot conceal from you that such an occasion as this produces within me feelings of sincere regret, for I know that our association together, as public servants, now practically ceases—an association that has been fraught with pleasant recollections of the work in which we were engaged. If I was able to be of use to you in any way, it is so long since, and the occasions were so infrequent, that I had forgotten it ; and now, no one familiar with the efficient manner in which your duties are performed, could suppose that you need aid or suggestions from any one. I am happy to acknowledge your courteous and unremitting kindness to me personally, and the great satisfaction I have had in my necessary official intercourse with you for many years. It is well when public officers, who are in close and intimate relation of duty, are able to work harmoniously together. It is satisfactory to themselves. It is a benefit to the public. That satisfaction I have shared without a single drawback, and am bold to say nowhere have the public been more faithfully and zealously served than in this extensive and populous jurisdiction. The very best officers are liable to have their acts misunderstood and their services under-rated, and they are sometimes called upon to stand upon their defence. I cannot recollect, however, a single instance in which a well-grounded complaint against any one of you came under my notice, and I am glad to bear testimony to the faithful, careful and discreet way in which your duties were ever performed.

I can say, without flattery, that our officials stand in knowledge, character and ability, second to none in the Province. If God grant that I return with renewed health, I hope to find congenial work of some kind for the good of our country, and possibly I may at times put on my old harness, and I am sure I should enjoy, as in the past, our communion of work ; but the strong motive for work that I had in the past will not be there, for I feel that my object has now been attained, and my able successors will well and faithfully carry on the work that, as chief magistrate, I inaugurated, and which has been brought to a fair state of completeness through the very efficient help that has been accorded to me.

I need not allude, in detail, to the many kind things you have said of me in your address. You have given me something by which to remember you in the days to come, when I shall not meet you in daily converse ; but partings are sad, and I do not feel equal to more extended remarks.

I thank you for myself and my wife, for your kind wish in reference to our journey. I will only add that each of you possesses my warm regard, and that I part from you, I hope only for a short time, with earnest wishes for your well being, in both your official and private lives. I bid you a warm farewell.

Mr. Adam Dudgeon, Mayor of Collingwood, and Clerk of the Fourth Division Court, then advanced to the table followed by a large number of the officers present, and read the following address, to His Honor :

We, the officers of the Division Courts of the county of Simcoe, feel that, after so many years of official and personal intercourse with you, it would be impossible for us to permit the occasion of your retirement from active service to pass without giving some formal expression to our sentiments. We regret very deeply that you have found it necessary to resign the position of Senior Judge of the county, which you have so worthily and acceptably filled for so long a period. We desire to express our gratitude to you for the many acts of kindness and attention which we have received at your hands in the direction of our official duties. We have never sought advice or instruction from you in vain, but we have always found you to be ready and willing to assist us in every way to perform our duties, and full of solicitude for the best interests of both officers and suitors. The relations between a Judge and his subordinate officers are not always of the most friendly description, and it gives us unfeigned satisfaction to be able to bear our unanimous testimony to the unvarying kindness and courteous consideration with which you have at all times treated the Division Court officials of the county. We are firmly of opinion that a great part of the success which has attended the administration of justice in the " People's Court" of this county, is owing to your jealous care and supervision, and to the signal ability with which you have conducted their affairs. As a very slight token of our esteem and regard, we cordially beg your acceptance of the accompanying small gift [a handsome gold-headed cane, on which was engraved His Honor's name, etc.], and it is our earnest hope that your future life may be fully laden with all possible happiness and comfort."

In reply, His Honor expressed his regret that the intimation of this address and presentation came too late for him to write his reply, but his thanks, he said, were none the less hearty and sincere. He had appointed over one hundred subordinate officials (only four of whom he had had occasion to remove), and many of whom had since been appointed to responsible positions in the county and Province. He had looked only to personal fitness in all his appointments. The law was, however, now changed, and all such appointments were vested in the Government of the day, and although they had, of course, a much more limited field to select from, he hoped the best available men would be chosen to fill the subordinate Division Court offices, as had been the case in the late appointments. Formerly, those who held these offices received large fees, but now their emoluments were reduced to the lowest living point. But he hoped the law would be so amended as to supplement these fees by a small salary. His Honor concluded by again thanking them for the good wishes expressed in the address just read, and the accompanying beautiful present.*

The piece of plate referred to in the address from the Bar, Mr. Lount explained, could not be procured in time. It was subsequently obtained in England † from "The Goldsmith and Silversmith Manufacturing Company," Regent Street, London, and is a very beautiful work of art. It is in the form of a silver centre-piece, designed in the Greco-Roman style of art. From a handsome triangular base, richly decorated with shields, enriched with the maple leaf and bearing the Arms of Canada and of the Province of Ontario, as well as a design from the Arms of the Law Society of Ontario, and the recipient's own Arms, springs three columns supporting a canopy, under which stands a majestic figure of Justice. From the centre of the canopy spring three richly wrought branches and a centre stem, each supporting glass dishes for fruit and flowers.

---

* " Examiner," 18th October, 1883.

† The Bar were fortunate enough to secure the valuable aid of James Hore, Esq., of Drinagh, Dulwich, England, himself a retired Judge of the Indian Bench, in carrying out their intention in respect to the testimonial, and that gentleman, who is a connection of Senator Gowan, most kindly in their behalf, arranged with the manufacturers as to the design and execution.

On one of the shields is the inscription : " Presented by the Bar of the Judicial District of Simcoe, to His Honor Judge Gowan, on the occasion of his retirement from the Bench, as a mark of their appreciation of long and valuable public services and as a token of their personal esteem and regard. Barrie, 16th October, 1883."

The cane presented by the Division Court officers was unique, of its kind the finest that could be procured in the country, and the solid gold head bore the following inscription : " Presented to His Honor Judge Gowan, on his retiring from the Bench, by the Division Court officers, county of Simcoe."

After the ceremony had closed, the Judge received the warm greeting of his friends, and bade good-bye to those present.

The whole scene was touching and interesting ; it was the severing of a connection of over forty years, with the spontaneous testimony, of those best capable of forming an opinion, to a well-spent life—to the employment, continuous and persevering, of rare abilities in the faithful discharge of duty—to abundant and successful effort to promote the public good.*

---

* In referring to Judge Gowan's career in Canada, a prominent Dublin journal, "The Irish Times," thus concludes a leading article: "We recognize in the life-work and brilliant success of our brother Irishman, another proof that in the Colonial field Irish success often eclipses that of men of every other nationality, and earns for our people a higher regard in the world. Judge Gowan's scholarship and literary skill, added to his legal qualities, have rendered him one of the most accomplished jurists of Canada throughout many years."

A leading local journal, referring to Judge Gowan at this time, happily said : "No man in the length and breadth of the land was better known.

The sentiments expressed in the addresses were not, as has been said before, mere words of compliment, they were evoked by facts ; and moreover, Judge Gowan had won the respect and attachment of those with whom he had been in contact for many years.

The Judge left for England the day after the presentation of these addresses. The first meeting of Simcoe Municipal Council took place at Barrie, the following month. This " House of Representatives," composed of over fifty Reeves and Deputy-Reeves, elected by an annual vote of the registered voters in the several municipalities in Council, unanimously expressed their regret at Judge Gowan's retirement, and determined that an address from their body should follow him to England, and that the Council should otherwise mark their high estimation of the Judge. Finally, it was determined that his likeness should be procured * and hung in the Council Chamber in the Court House, where the session of the Council is held, and where, when the Civil and Criminal

---

The old Judge, as he was familiarly called, has been a prominent figure for half a century, the venerated Chief Magistrate of two generations. His high legal attainments and keen perceptive faculties were not alone appreciated by the Bar, the whole country understood and valued his great industry and ability, another instance of the vigor and intelligence of the Celtic race. Like Lord Brougham, with a wealth of legal lore he possessed also a highly cultivated mind, and did his part amongst us in the advancement of learning, science and art, at once the true patron of the student and a most distinguished Judge."

* The deputation appointed to pronounce upon the fidelity of the likeness consisted of His Worship the Warden; Colonel Banting, County Clerk; O. J. Phelps, Esq., M.P.P.; G. P. McKay, Esq., M.P.P.; Charles Drury, Esq., M.P.P.; Henry H. Hammell, Esq., M.P.P.; William Lount, Esq., Q.C.

business of the Courts was occasionally divided, Judge Gowan usually sat.

Not long after, the address, in album form, bound in high art style, and richly and beautifully illuminated, followed the Judge to the Old Country, and it must have been more than gratifying to him, a stranger and sojourner in the "Old Land," to receive this token of remembrance from his far off home.

The address from the Warden and Members of the Council, after referring to the Judge's retirement, declared " they could not allow the event to pass without giving some expression of their very high appreciation, not only of the many kindly services willingly rendered them during that lengthened period, but of the great interest at all times taken by you in the public affairs of the county, and more particularly of the assistance given in bringing the Municipal Laws of the Province to their present state of great efficiency, and also in the consolidation and revision of the general laws of this Province. And the members of this council have always felt a just pride in the knowledge of having one to refer to in any matter of importance, and one so willing to give his best assistance at all times."

"When a man has given the best years of his life to the service of his country—and particularly in such an arduous position as you occupied for many years, in the earlier days, after your appointment as Judge, when the country was sparsely settled, and roads often next to impassable, and even the common comforts of life not attainable—the least those who enjoy the fruits of your labor can do, is in some way to recognize those services."

" The County Council, as a very small recognition of your services to that body, have determined to place a well-executed and framed likeness of your Honor in the Council Chamber over the seat you have so long honorably and efficiently filled ; and they trust you will approve of this simple tribute to your worth, not only as a public man, but as a citizen of this county, in the spirit in which it is done."

"We cannot close this address without wishing yourself and Mrs. Gowan all the health, happiness and prosperity that it is possible for any of us to enjoy in this life ; and long may you both be spared in God's good providence to enjoy the wide-spread reputation you have so well and faithfully earned by a long life of hard and continuous work."

The Judge's reply was subsequently laid before the Council, and appears in the minutes of the following session. It is as follows :

To the Worshipful Warden and Members of the County Council of the County of Simcoe,—

GENTLEMEN,—Your address has followed me to the Old Land, far away from the dear home where so many happy years of my life were spent amongst you all. Such unexpected kindness touches me deeply, and no language can convey my sincere appreciation of your approving testimony.

The governing body in the largest and most prosperous county in Ontario, and I might add in the Dominion, representing not merely its municipal powers, but its intelligence, its agricultural, commercial, manufacturing and professional interests, I may well feel honored in having received such an address from gentlemen whose position commands respect for their testimony ; and, although there may be an element of personal kindness in your action, I trust I may regard it as a deliberate expression of opinion that I have not been wanting in an earnest endeavor to discharge my duty faithfully, that I have not been unmindful that it became me to assist, according to my opportunities, in all that was calculated to promote the solid good of those amongst whom my lot was cast.

I certainly have from the first been somewhat familiar with our district Councils, and although I recognized imperfection in the new scheme, I never faltered in the conviction that the advantages of safe self-government would ultimately be abundantly manifest. I was not mistaken. We can now fairly claim that we possess the most perfect system of municipal government enjoyed by any country and have proved that an intelligent and educated people may be safely entrusted with the management of important matters demanding local administration—matters that would but retard and embarrass the proceedings of the higher legislative bodies, if, indeed, they were *there* able to secure the attentions they deserved.

The large powers you possess could, however, as I think we feel, only be safely entrusted to fit and capable agents, and you will agree with me that our excellent school system has played an important part in producing the state of perfection in working to which our municipal system has attained. The very small aid I have been able to

give towards its safe development, would have had no
practical result, if the public men who, from time to time,
shaped legislation, had not themselves earnestly desired
to make our municipal law what it is ; or if the County
Councils lacked the discretion and intelligence necessary
for the due performance of their important and responsible
duties.

I have always been proud of the high position of your
body amongst the Councils of the Province, and not one
of them has furnished more conspicuous evidence of the
educating value of such bodies in fitting men for the
higher duties of representatives of the people in the Legislature.

In many respects our county stands foremost, and having watched its progress from the primitive condition of a
"new settlement," I am filled with admiration of the
patient industry and intelligent energy that have accomplished so much in a period of forty-one years. You know
that at first we had barely passable roadways through the
" woods," that farming operations were conducted in a
very imperfect way, that commerce and manufactures were
scarcely in the bud, that the few schools which existed
were imperfectly served and ill-regulated, while the municipal system was a recent creation, and, moreover, that
ready submission to the law of the land was *not* universal.
Many of you will remember the time when this state of
things prevailed, and will know what a contrast presents
itself as you now look around you—the whole country
accessible by excellent roads, and more than that, netted
all over with railroads, agriculture in its various aspects

carried on intelligently by an educated farming community, free public schools, with efficient teachers under a uniform system, within easy access of all, the laws everywhere respected and cheerfully obeyed, and last, though not least, our municipal system permeating every part with its healthy influences—yes, when you look around you you cannot help feeling that ours is a happy and honorable position, and must bless God every day that your lot is cast in a free country, where there is work for all, and bread for all; where honest labor meets its appropriate reward, and where any deserving man in the community may aspire to the highest place and the largest power for serving his country.

If we have contentions and some acerbity of feelings at times, I fear they are inseparable from our form of party government; but I do earnestly hope that, whatever divergence may exist in matters of political concern, all will continue to be united in the effort to maintain and improve the prosperous and honorable position in which the county of Simcoe now stands.

The particular mode in which you have been pleased to recognize my desire to be useful is very grateful to my feelings, and I thank you sincerely for the honor you have done me in placing my likeness in your Council Chamber, and in voting me your kind address in such beautiful form.

Mrs. Gowan cordially thanks you for including her in your kind wishes, which we both warmly reciprocate.

My earnest wish is that wisdom may direct all your deliberations, and strengthen you in every effort for the public good ; **above all**, I desire that each of you individually, may possess the blessing which maketh **rich and** addeth no sorrow with it.

Believe me, most faithfully yours,

JAS. ROBERT GOWAN.

Kensington House, Bournemouth,
Hants, England, February 2, 1884.

The Judge's likeness, extremely well-executed, now occupies the place of honor mentioned in the address of the Council.

The University of Queen's College, at Convocation, in its forty-third session, in 1884, while Mr. Gowan was in England, conferred upon him the honorary degree of LL.D. This marked recognition of worth by a great university, very sparing of the distinctions she confers,* was a compliment indeed, and must have been most gratifying to the Judge, as it certainly was to his friends in Canada and elsewhere. A leading Old Country paper, "The Irish Times," thus refers to the matter : "We are gratified to find in the Toronto 'Mail,' of the 1st of May, a report of proceedings of peculiar interest in the Convocation Hall of the University of Queen's, when the degrees were conferred and prizes distributed to a large number of successful students. One of the most striking features of the occasion

---

* Up to that time the distinction had been conferred on merely thirteen laymen, namely : "The Marquis of Lorne, Sir John A. Macdonald, The Honorable Oliver Mowat, Robert Bell, M.D., Edward J. Chapman, Alexander F. Kemp, Peter McLaren, George Romanes, William Tassie, John Thorburn, Alpheus Todd, George Paxton Young, and Sir William Young.

was the giving of an honorary degree to Judge Gowan, a distinguished Irishman, whose career in Canada has been most successful. The honor thus paid to Judge Gowan, in recognition of his high abilities and long service in the judiciary, will not fail to be appreciated by his countrymen."

We make an extract from the report of the proceedings at convocation, published in the Toronto "Globe":

"Vice-Principal Williamson then advanced, and moved to have the names of three eminent gentlemen added to the list of those bearing honorary titles conferred by this University. In doing so, he moved the following three addresses:

" Mr. Vice-Chancellor,—

" I have the honor to present to you the name of Judge James Robert Gowan, as one on whom the Senate desires to confer the degree of LL.D., in special recognition of great public services, in connection with our judicial system, the codification of our laws, and the educational and religious life of our country. It is scarcely possible to over-estimate the value of Judge Gowan's services, continued unwearily for nearly half a century, particularly as regards procedure in Courts, and the revision, consolidation and classification of the Statutes, first of Upper Canada, and subsequently of Ontario. For his labors in this latter work, it may be mentioned that he was presented with a gold medal by the Government of Ontario. His literary labors, and the many important and official positions he has held, have not prevented him from undertaking other onerous duties to which the voice of his fellow-citizens called him, and in the discharge of which he has displayed the highest qualities of a good citizen and of an earnest catholic Christian. He has acted for more than thirty years as Chairman of the High School Board of the county of Simcoe, has aided to the uttermost of his ability every good cause, and has endeared himself to his colleagues and the public by varied abilities, untiring industry, and sterling character."

In one of the addresses presented to Mr. Gowan on his retirement it was said :

"We feel satisfied, notwithstanding your retirement from the Bench, that your matured knowledge will not be lost to the country, but that in some shape the community will yet have the benefit of the vast amount of experience that you have acquired during so long and active a public life." This expression proved to be a correct forecast. Mr. Gowan left for Europe immediately after his retirement, returning in the autumn of 1884. He was not long allowed to remain in private life, for within three months after his return he was recalled to the service of his country in another field, receiving the Queen's summons to the Senate of Canada.

"The Senate of Canada stands in the same relation to the other House as the House of Lords to the Commons in England," and the body possessses the independent power and privileges of an Upper Chamber as a constituent part of the Parliament of Canada. The appointment of Senators is for life. The position of a Senator is therefore properly regarded as the most honorable distinction that

can be conferred in this Dominion.* Indeed, the idea, as
well as the intention, of a second chamber would seem to
be, that such body should comprehend men of high character and position, representing the professional and other
prominent classes—men of mature judgment, animated by
zeal for the public interests, rather than party attachments
—men of independent means. In a word, educated, grave,
fair-minded men, imbued with a high sense of honor and
true national spirit—" of the people and from the people,"
and possessing a deep stake in the welfare of the country.

The appointment was offered to Mr. Gowan in a very
kind and graceful communication from Sir John Macdonald,† and accepted. "I determined," Mr. Gowan said,
in answer to one of the addresses to him, "with some
misgivings, to accept, for I could only bring to the place
a residuum of former energy, and much could not be
expected in a man not very far from three score and ten."

The appointment, the highest distinction the Government could confer, was most favorably commented on by

---

* By " The Table of Precedence within the Dominion of Canada," Senators take rank before the Speaker of the Commons, and before the Puisne
Judges of the Courts of Law and Equity.

† The Premier wrote Mr. Gowan : " At last the opportunity has arrived,
for which I have long waited, of being able to offer you a Senatorship.

" That august body is greatly in want of legal ability, and Campbell knows
from me of what value you have been to me in years gone by. McPherson,
you well know, is pleased with the suggestion, so is Frank Smith. When the
appointment (if you accept it, which I earnestly hope you will) is announced,
it will be put upon the ground of the great benefit it will be to the public to
have an experienced *juris consult* like you in the Upper House * * . Telegraph me ' Yes ' or ' No,' and be sure to say ' Yes.'"

the public press of all shades. "The Week," a thoroughly
independent journal, and one of the ablest and best conducted on the continent, in its issue of the 5th February,
1885, thus referred to the nomination :—"Judge Gowan is
a personal and political friend of Sir John Macdonald, but
he has never taken an active part in politics, nor can his
appointment be fairly said to be the reward of partizanship.
By his long service in the judiciary, and by his liberal and
comprehensive view of law, as well as by his character and
position, he is well fitted to represent his profession in the
Senate, and to play a useful part in moulding legislation,
and especially in the codification of the law. The selection
was as creditable as any selection could be in which party
lines were not entirely ignored. We hailed it as a new
departure, and began to surmise that beneficent influence
might have been exercised in a quiet way by the Governor-
General, who is ostensibly responsible, and to whom, in an
hour so critical for second chambers, the condition of the
Canadian House of Lords must be far from a pleasant
spectacle." And in a later issue, this journal, while object-
ing to "investing men with legislative powers for life as
rewards for party services which were not also services to
the country," adds, "Mr. Gowan's services were services to
the country."

The "Canada Law Journal" thus commented upon the
nomination: "The appointment has been accepted by parties of all shades of politics as creditable to the Government
of the day and an honor deservedly bestowed on a faithful
servant of our country. * * We look upon this appointment as the establishing of a happy precedent. A retired

Judge in many instances will preserve sufficient mental vigor and physical strength to discharge the duties of a legislator—especially in the less partizan atmosphere of the Upper Chamber of our Dominion Parliament. The appointment of Judge Gowan opens up a new and useful field for men of this class, in which the ripened experience and trained abilities of some of our ablest judicial minds may find congenial occupation, and at the same time afford an honorable and fitting termination to many eminent careers."

" No one will question the eminent fitness of His Honor Judge Gowan to be a Senator of the Dominion, even though that body were the most important branch of our legislative system. His known ability as a jurist, and his intimate acquaintance with all the varied needs of this great country, peculiarly fit him for senatorial honors, or to hold a portfolio in some government. And although it is many a long year since Senator Gowan took any part in Canadian politics, he has, as his friends are well aware, kept abreast with the times, and is really better posted on the leading political and social issues of the day than many an M.P. or M.P.P. He has had, too, the advantage of having been able to take a dispassionate view of all questions before the country ; and in this respect, as in some others, Senator Gowan will compare favorably with ' Bystander' in the view he takes of the measures agitating the country, for his mental vision is not obscured by Old Country notions or prejudices. He is gifted with a robust intellect, and so can never become a mere party man. He will, in fact, be as much an ornament of the Senate as he has been of the Bench these forty years past. We heartily congratulate Judge Gowan on his appointment to the Senate, and hope he may be spared many years to do the country further service in his new sphere of usefulness."

The foregoing is from "The Examiner," the leading local Opposition journal in Simcoe. "The Manitoba Free Press," also an Opposition journal, after a brief sketch of Mr. Gowan's career, says: "He is credited with being the author of a large amount of useful legislation before and since Confederation; and is known to have more than once declined removal to the Upper Bench. He has always had the goodwill of, and possessed influence with, every Government, local or general, which has been in power since his appointment. * * His ability as a jurist and his general practical knowledge of business, and latterly his long experience, added to a great capacity for work, have in many instances enabled him to render valuable service to the Government of the day, and to the country.

"His call to the Senate must be looked upon as a recognition of merit rather than a political appointment Judge Gowan's politics, when he was in a position to have any, being evidently (judging by his appointment) Baldwinite, or Reform. Judge Gowan is said to be still full of mental vigor, and it is almost to be regretted that his talents as a legislator could not have been called into requisition in a more congenial atmosphere than that of the Senate Chamber. Judge Gowan has on many occasions during his judicial career, as well as at its close, been the recipient of flattering but well-merited indications of the high esteem and appreciation in which he was held by the Bar, and the people of the county in which he resided."

" It is almost unnecessary to add," said " The Toronto Mail," "that his elevation will give universal satisfaction; a profound and experienced lawyer, he also possesses a wide acquaintance with all the leading issues of the day."

" There is not a man in the Dominion," said " The Barrie Advance," "better fitted to do the duties of a Senator and to add dignity to the second Chamber.   *   * His scholarly bearing, his vast legal attainments, and the dignity and suavity of his manner, will make Judge Gowan a real acquisition in the Canadian House of Lords."

" The two latest appointments to the Senate were not made from the ranks of the professional politicians, and that is at least something in their favor.   One was a judge and the other a doctor, and so long as the Senate must continue to be constituted on the nominative principle the nominations should be made, as much as possible, from the ranks of the professional or mercantile classes.   The country will thus be able to secure the services of representative men.   Judge Gowan has done yeoman service on the Bench, and his long and faithful discharge of judicial duties deserves some such mark of national appreciation as that which has been conferred upon him.   Dr. Sullivan, of Kingston, is one of the most popular Catholics in the country, and his elevation to the Senate will be especially acceptable to that section of the community." This is from a journal opposed to an appointed Senate.

Another strong Opposition local paper, "The Times," declared : " No more popular selection could have been made for this district. Had the office been elective, the leading men of both political parties would have united in choosing the Judge. He will honor the Senate, by becoming one of its number, more than that august body will honor him by receiving him as one of its members. Had Sir John A. Macdonald been equally happy in his selection of Senators, as in the case of his first appointment from this county, the outcry against the Senate as a refuge for broken-down politicians would have been groundless. This most fitting appointment is, moreover, an incentive to our young men to be active and energetic in the position into which the great Creator has put them."

After referring to Mr. Gowan's appointment to the Bench at the early age of twenty-four, and his long and earnest labors, especially to make the Courts as easy to the poor man as to the rich, the journal we quote adds: "And now, in his declining years, with his natural powers as vigorous as ever, honors are heaped upon him, which are the more valuable, because they are richly deserved. Our sincere wish is that the venerable Judge may be spared for many years, to enjoy the rewards of his past labors and efforts to do good."

Only one leading journal, " The Toronto Globe," spoke in non-approving terms of the appointment. " We do not know that any remarks need be made on these Tory appointments, except that it is remarkable to find a gentleman unable, because of infirmity, to retain his seat on the Bench, selected for the Senate." This statement refers to Mr. Gowan, but is neither fair nor correct. It was not because the Judge was "unable, because of infirmity, to retain his seat on the Bench" that he sought retirement— though his tenure of office was for a longer period of actual service than that of any other Judge in any Colony of the Empire, fifteen years beyond the time he might have retired under the Statute. Indeed, he probably might have gone on for years at the full salary for such work as he was able to do. His own explanation, as we already know, given in reply to the Bar address in 1883, is: "Let me say one word as to my retirement. As you are aware, this is the largest judicial district in the Province, having a population, not very long since, equal to that of Manitoba and British Columbia together. The duties are very onerous, requiring the services of at least two active men to perform properly, with the promptitude demanded in the various duties made incident to the Judge's office. And I felt the time had come when, in justice to the public and my brother Judges, I should make way for a younger man. My age and uncertain health demanded more repose than I could properly ask or take, and so I sought retirement. And after forty-one years of hard work, it cannot be said that my appeal to be relieved was in any sense premature. Indeed, I have the satisfaction of knowing that His Excellency appreciates, as he is pleased to communicate, my faithful, efficient and impartial conduct during my long term of judicial service;" and continuing, "Should I return, as I trust I shall, with restored health, I hope to find some opening for usefulness, for I feel that I am not without a a residuum of energy, and I could not live an idle life." And that Mr. Gowan was willing, at an advanced age, to give his services to the country for some months every year is all to his credit. It is scarcely necessary to say anything of his mental fitness for the duties of a Senator. As expressed by leading Liberal journals in his own district : "Mr. Gowan's natural powers are as vigorous as ever, * * of his fitness for the position there is but one opinion, that of his being thoroughly competent." And his record during the first session he attended, sustains the correctness of these assertions.

The "Canada Educational Monthly" spoke also of the appointment as exceedingly popular, and referred to it as "an event of interest to all friends of education. The new Senator can probably claim to have served longer as a school trustee than any other man in the Province. He was, we believe, a member of the original Board of Grammar School Trustees at Barrie, more than forty years ago, and he is to-day the respected chairman of the Collegiate Institute of that town."

One quotation more may be made from "The Irish Times" of February 19th, a leading paper in Mr. Gowan's native country. "It is with much satisfaction we learn from the journals of Canada, received by the mail delivered yesterday, that, on the 3rd of the present month, a distinguished Irish jurist, who had before attained the highest distinction in Canada, for many years in a judicial capacity, and more lately as a principal commissioner for the codifying of the laws of the Dominion, has been raised to the dignity of the Senate of Canada by command of Her Majesty. The Honorable James Robert Gowan, is a native of the county of Wexford, and a gentleman of genius and experience. * * The universal respect in which the new Senator is held, and his conspicuous fitness for the Council room of a great State, must be a matter of pleasing record for all Irishmen who delight to hear of the superior display of talent and energy by their country-men abroad, of the success which attends them in the noblest walks of life, and the usefulness to society of the career in which they have risen to eminence."

Mr. Gowan heard also from a number of old friends in congratulation.*

Amongst the congratulations offered to the newly ap-pointed Senator, there was one that seems to call for a fuller notice, namely, the address from the Council—the

---

* Some of these letters have already been referred to, and we give some more. They are taken from a paper printed some two years ago, for private circulation, by a relative of Senator Gowan, who explained that he had been permitted to make selections from numerous unpublished letters addressed to the Senator on his retirement from the Bench, as well as on his appointment to the Senate, and were given without standing on any order of arrangement :

LETTERS ON THE OCCASION OF HIS RETIREMENT FROM THE BENCH.

From the Minister of Justice, Sir Alex. Campbell, 21st September, 1883.

"I reported yesterday on your resignation, and the appointment of your successor, but Sir John [The Premier] added, with his own hand, some complimentary remarks to the Order-in-Council for transmission to His Excel-lency ; need I say how heartily I approved. For over forty years the country has had the benefit of your faithful service in the honorable position you adorned, and you have well earned your retirement. When the Order-in-Council returns from His Excellency I shall have pleasure in transmitting to you some note of this exceptional expression."

The Premier of Canada, Sir John A. Macdonald, 28th September.

"Your letter announcing your resignation reached here on the day I was leaving for Kingston to see my sister, then supposed to be in great danger.

great representative body of the judicial district in which
he has resided for so many years. And the following
account is condensed from reports of public journals, representing both political parties in the county.

"The Council lost no time in congratulating His Honor
Judge Gowan on his elevation to the Senate. A special
committee was struck to frame an address as soon as it
became known that the appointment had been made. It
was carried by acclamation, and the Council then adjourned
till four o'clock in the afternoon of the same day, the 6th
February, 1885. At the hour named the Council assem-
bled, and shortly after the newly appointed Senator and
ex-Judge entered the Council Chamber, and was conducted

I went to the Council, however, so as to sign the order accepting your resignation. You will see there a just tribute to your long and faithful judicial
service. So far as I know, this is the only instance in which such a testimonial
has been given to any Judge of any Court, but you have well earned the thanks
of the Government and the community.

"I have pleasant recollections of our intimate personal relations for many
years back, and a grateful sense of the great assistance you gave me in the
preparation of matters both legislative and administrative. Relieved now from
the cares of official life, you will be better able to take care of your health
* * .

"I hope on your return next year to be able to see much of you, and
perhaps to engage you in some congenial work for the good of our country"
* * .

The Honorable J. H. Hagarty, Chief Justice of Ontario, 25th September.

"I have no shadow of doubt you have acted wisely in abandoning the
duties that you have so efficiently performed for forty-one years. I wish that
others had as fair a record and could as reasonably look forward to retire
amidst sincere regret as will greet your resignation.

"I congratulate you that, unlike many others, you have not to cling to
official duties because you cannot afford to abandon them * * all health
and happiness in his well-earned leisure to 'the friend of my better days.'"

to a seat beside the Warden ; the members and numerous visitors rising at his entrance. The address was read by the Warden, as follows :

"'We, the members of the County Council of the county of Simcoe, have heard with extreme gratification that you have been called to the Senate of the Dominion of Canada, and we cannot allow the occasion to pass without extending to you our sincere congratulations on the high honor you have received. We feel, both personally and collectively, that no better selection could have been made, and we heartily trust that you may be spared health and many years to enjoy your proud position. We venture to express the opinion that the intention of the founders of our Senate

---

The Honorable J. G. Spragge, Chief Justice of Appeal (formerly Chancellor) for Ontario, 2nd October.

" You certainly have earned retirement, if long, faithful and efficient service can entitle any man to it ; but I am sorry if impaired health had anything to do with your leaving the judicial seat which you have filled with honor for so many years. We are both veterans in the public service. You with a judicial life longer than mine. You retire with the regret of those you leave behind * * My friends tell me I should not be happy if I had not work to do. Perhaps so, but I would fain try. I fancy that you and I have resources enough to prevent our dying of *ennui*. I hope most sincerely you may enjoy your *otium cum dignitate* for a long time, and that rest and change may restore you to vigorous health.

Chief Justice Sir Adam Wilson, 9th October.

" I see by the papers you have retired from the Bench, after a service of the longest judicial term of any one in any part of the Dominion, and I might safely allow a far more extended area. C. J. Bowen was nominally on the Bench for fifty years, but for at least ten years before his death never sat ; substantially, then, you are the longest holder of judicial rank that I know of who has discharged the actual duties of his office during the whole period of his term. You have earned your retirement well, and have earned it long ago,

has been fully carried out in the elevation to that distinguished assembly of so eminent a public servant as yourself. You will bring to that body a mind highly cultivated and trained by a judicial experience of more than forty years, and never having taken a prominent part in the political warfare of the country, you will adjudicate on matters brought under your notice impartially and without bias. Having assisted in the consolidation of our laws and been instrumental in framing many of our Statutes which, by their permanence on the Statute book, testify to the thoroughness and foresight with which they are framed, it may safely be predicted that, in your new and exalted sphere; the country will gain the benefit of your

---

and all who know you will wish that you may long enjoy the repose you are so well entitled to. I am sure the methodical arrangements you had adopted and enforced from all your subordinate officers, had a very beneficial effect on them as well as others who saw its working and were brought into personal contact with yourself * * . It is wonderful what the one man can do who has devoted himself to his work and understands what he is about. Your decisions were very, very rarely up in appeal, the best evidence that they were sound and satisfactory. I do not know if any of them have been overruled, and if they had, it would not be an infallible test of their unsoundness. And now, my dear Gowan, while bidding you farewell as a brother Judge, I hope we may ever continue our friendship."

Sir William B. Richards, formerly Chief Justice of Ontario, afterwards Chief Justice of the Supreme Court of Canada, 5th November.

"I first learned here [New York] of your resignation of the position you have so long held with credit to yourself and advantage to the country.

"We hear a good deal of men dying in harness, and, no doubt, many holding the judicial office have done so ; but after a man has worked as hard and as faithfully as you have done for more than forty years, he has the right to seek relaxation ; if his health requires his giving up work, so much the stronger reason for his doing so.

matured experience in compiling other enactments equally advantageous to our Dominion at large.

"'We have no doubt that the Chamber that you are now henceforth to occupy, will not only receive additional lustre from your presence, but that your wise counsel and clear intelligence will mould their discussions and affect the result of their deliberations in a marked and beneficial degree.

"'As representatives of this large district, we feel a pride reflecting that the advice and counsel you always so freely accorded us, and which we were always willing to be guided by, have been recognized to be of such worth—recognized by the highest authorities of the State. And we trust that

---

"You may properly feel proud, not only of your able and energetic discharge of judicial duty—well warranting the reputation you obtained for sound judgment and efficient service—but also of the voluntary and patriotic aid you were willing and able to lend public men in preparing and revisin important measures of law reform, as I very well know" * *.

The Honorable J. W. Gwynne, Justice Supreme Court of Canada, 26th September.

"I congratulate you on your retirement into your well earned *otium cum dignitate.* * * And so you are going to England; you will, I trust, not cut Canada altogether. I sincerely hope you will enjoy in improved health, that leisure which your long and distinguished labors in discharge of your judicial duties so richly entitle you to. Few men can look back with equal satisfaction on the useful and varied labors of their life. Long, my dear friend, may you live to enjoy your retirement."

The Honorable Sir Oliver Mowat, Attorney-General for Ontario, 27th September.

"I am extremely sorry you have felt occasion to resign your Judgeship. I do hope the rest will add to your life many additional years of comfort. I will have great pleasure in continuing you as Chairman of the Board of Judges [as a retired Judge he was eligible] and perhaps I may be selfish enough to

the wise and prudent advice so inculcated may ever be handed down to future representatives as a priceless tradition, never to be forgotten.'

"The Senator replied verbally, with a good deal of feeling—naturally, for he stood in the presence of prominent men who had known him for years, amongst whom he had spent the greater part of his life, and fulfilled the duties of the judicial position. He returned sincere and hearty thanks for the honor, said it was specially gratifying in view of its being unanimous, and because it represented, even in committee, men of various political convictions coming from all sections of the district. The Senator, continuing, said :

---

ask your counsel and assistance occasionally in other matters. With thanks for your good offices in the past, and my best wishes for the happiness of you and yours, believe me," etc.

Mr. Goldwin Smith, D.C.L., 27th September.

" * * With the rest of your friends, and with all those among whom your long life of usefulness and honor has been passed, I shall deplore the necessity of your retirement from the Bench ; yet I cannot doubt you have done right. An evening of rest and calm never was better earned by a long day of good work than it has been in your case. I have never heard any opinion but one on that subject. If party could let politicians listen to the voice of justice, the acceptance of your resignation as Judge would be followed, as soon as possible, by an offer of a place in the Senate."

Mr. G. W. Wickstead, Q.C., Law Clerk House of Commons, with whom Mr. Gowan had long association in the work of Statutory Consolidation and Drafting, 28th September.

" I congratulate you, but not the country or the profession, that you have decided to sue out your writ of ease" * * . No one will envy you the blessings to which your unique services, in quantity and quality, for forty-one years, more than entitle you. I am gratified in having my name coupled with yours as having done the State some service. You might truly, as to yourself,

"'*Mr. Warden and Gentlemen,*—

"'I would gladly take you into my confidence if I had anything to impart; but you know almost as much as I do in respect to my appointment. On Monday last, I had the first intimation that it was desired I should take a place in the Senate. It was wholly unexpected by me, and I need scarcely say I never sought it. The offer was entirely spontaneous, and after seeing the few friends I could consult—seeing that a prompt answer was necessary —I determined, with some misgiving, to accept, for I could only bring to the place a residuum of former energy, and much could not be expected in a man not very far from three-score years and ten.

---

say, 'and they know it!' Our relations in the past are not likely to be renewed, for I am a much older man than you, but I hope I may live to see you on your return from England, almost as good as new, as Sir John would say."

And from Sir Francis Hincks, the only survivor of the Baldwin-Lafontaine Government at the time of Mr. Gowan's appointment, 13th October.

"' * * I recollect both the Attorney and Solicitor-General being strongly for your appointment in 1842. The former (Honorable Robert Baldwin) speaking favorably of your legal fitness and sound judgment. I well remember his saying, though you were young, you would do credit to the judicial office. He was right, as your career has proved. Your tenure of office was not as long as C. J. Bowen's, but for years before his death he was useless, and it was difficult to get him to accept his pension. That cannot be said of you."

LETTERS ON THE OCCASION OF MR. GOWAN'S APPOINTMENT TO THE SENATE.

The Honorable J. Patton, leader of the Bar in Mr. Gowan's Courts when elected to Upper House, afterwards Solicitor-General and Member of the Senate, 28th January.

"To-day's 'Mail' announces your appointment to the Senate; I hasten to congratulate you on the high honor.

"'Why the appointment was offered to me I can only surmise. I had neither suffered nor bled in political warfare; had not even drawn the political sword. If, for a short time in early life, I was in the heat of a political blaze, more than forty years in the quiet shade was sufficient to remove dye or freckle. I had no claim of this kind to bring me into notice. Several members of the Government had known me for years, and I have for them a warm personal regard and respect, especially for Sir John Macdonald, with whom I had more contact and for whom I occasionally worked, as you know. But public men are not and ought not to be governed by personal feelings, and so I must surmise it was some supposed apti-

---

"Few men have done so much for their country by pen and speech as you during the past forty years, and the appointment will be welcomed as a deserving recognition of your great and philanthropic labors. Long may you enjoy your position in the Upper Chamber, as you will unquestionably shed a lustre on its debates and add to its usefulness * * .

"I could not resist writing to Sir John and telling him how well he had gauged public sentiment in seeking the benefit of your wise counsels, ripe and varied experience, and calm deliberate judgment."

Sir William B. Richards, Ex-Chief Justice Supreme Court of Canada, 20th February.

"I congratulate you upon your appointment, inasmuch as it affords you honorable employment in which your talents and experience will be usefully and profitably employed in the service of your country. Your appointment will be well received, it is just of the kind designed by the framers of the constitution in their aim to secure for the Second Chamber independent, thoughtful, representative men" * * .

In the April following, he again wrote the Senator.

"I see, by the reports, you are making yourself useful in the Senate, which needs the stimulus of active, energetic and practical men, who do not desire to work the political machine for personal or party objects."

tude for the position that influenced my selection. You
are good enough to think the intention of the founders of
the Senate is fully carried out by my appointment. I
hope you may be right. It is, at all events, most grateful
to me to know that the action of the Government, so far
as concerned me, meets your unqualified endorsation—a
most valuable endorsation it is, from the freely chosen
representatives of a district with a population, not very
long ago, exceeding that of two provinces in the Dominion,
and now not far behind that of Manitoba and British
Columbia together.

"'You are pleased to say I may have some influence in
the Senate. The utmost I hope for is to be of some use

Mr. Goldwin Smith, D.C.L., 21st February, wrote:

" ' ' You may be sure that, though many will rejoice, none will rejoice
more heartily than I do. This is indeed a new departure, and I only hope
there will not be a return to the old path. Reform, I have sometimes thought,
might make the Senate the better House of the two, but reform there must
be ! and, perhaps, when you and a few like you are there, there may be hopes
of that which now seems hopeless. The great drawback is the three months'
residence in Ottawa, but this to you will have its compensations " * * .

*And from Sir Matthew Cameron, Chief Justice Court Common Pleas, 25th
April.*

" ' ' Your appointment to the Senate gave me great satisfaction * * .
I was absent when the notice first appeared, but I hope you will permit me
now to say, your acceptance of this well-merited honor gave me the greatest
pleasure, in the assurance the country would be more to be congratulated than
yourself, as the gain would belong to it, while the trouble would be yours. I
hoped, however, that moulding our laws, as well as expounding them, might
form not a wholly uncongenial pursuit, and that you might derive some pleasure in the passing of laws, as the country derived benefit from your able exposition of them when on the Bench ; and that the leisure your retirement gave

in a quiet way, and as I fancy the best part of the work in deliberative bodies is done in committee, a place of usefulness may be found for me—it is my only aim and will be my reward. If I find in the body to which I shall have the honor to belong, as much earnest, well-directed effort as amongst you, I shall be content.'

" In conclusion, the new Senator again thanked them for their kind and courteous words, and their promptness in endorsing his appointment by valuable and deliberate testimony.

" The Honorable Senator, after greeting warmly several members of the Council, retired amid great cheering."

It was a magnificent and well-deserved ovation by men

---

you might thus be utilized in the promotion of your own enjoyment of your remaining years, as well as advancing the interests of the country."

Sir Oliver Mowat, Premier of Ontario, 3rd February, wrote :

" Your appointment gave me much pleasure. I have no doubt your presence in the Senate will be of great service to the public, and I hope you may find a couple of months every year attending Parliament to be agreeable to yourself, and that you may give many years to the active discharge of your Senatorial duties."

The Right Honorable Sir John Rose, some time Member of the Canadian Government, 20th February.

" * * I was much gratified in the announcement contained in the Senate minutes I received yesterday ; and I am equally pleased that our friend Sir John has so becomingly recognized your past services.

" I anticipate much advantage to the public interests from the matured judgment and good sense which you will bring to bear on all matters affecting the public interests.

" My sincere wish is that you may long live to enjoy your new position and add to your public usefulness."

of all parties, representatives of the people, to an eminent man who deserved well of his country—an honor few men could boast of, few could receive without being deeply touched.

It rarely falls to the lot of any one occupying a judicial position for over forty years to receive from public representatives of the people, men who knew him well, such a flattering demonstration of respect and regard. It may be mentioned that the address presented was subsequently

---

Mr. W. E. Hartpole Lecky, D.C.L., 21st February.

"I must congratulate you most sincerely on your new Senatorial dignity. It is a worthy crown of a long and honorable career, and I sincerely hope you may live long to enjoy it."

Sir Robert G. W. Herbert, Permanent Under Secretary for the Colonies, 20th April.

"I was much pleased to learn that you had been summoned to the Senate, and I feel that Canada is as much to be congratulated as yourself on the wise decision of Sir John Macdonald to make your great experience and sound judgment available to the public in this manner.

"I trust you may find opportunities for taking an active part in public business, as there are many matters in which your experience will enable you to be specially useful" * * .

The Most Honorable the Marquis of Dufferin and Ava, formerly Governor-General of Canada.

"I was glad of your kind thought in letting me know of your promotion to the Senate * * . I sincerely rejoice at your merits being so recognized. You have deserved well of your country, and of what can a man be prouder ; and in the Senate you will deserve better of it still" * * .

At a later date, His Lordship again wrote Mr. Gowan, from Simla, E.I.

"I am delighted to observe in how kind and proper a spirit your nomination has been received by the public. I shall always remember with pleasure my intercourse with you, and the firm and conscientious manner in which you discharged a distasteful duty under trying circumstances."

engrossed and illuminated in high art, in a magnificently bound album, and transmitted to Ottawa to Mr. Gowan. His acknowledgments, addressed to John Dickinson, Esq., Barrister, one of the reeves and chairman of the committee appointed to prepare the address, afterwards appeared in the journals of the Council.

"I never saw," said the Senator, "anything of the kind better done, or in better taste, both as regards binding and illumination. * * Sending it to me here has enabled me to show to Senators and others this mark of your regard. * * It was greatly and universally admired. Need I say 'the Senator from Barrie' was gratified in the fact. * * I have already told your body how much I was touched by their extreme kindness, but I should like them to know what I now say."

Authorities have frequently given their opinion upon the constitution of the Senate of Canada, and what, in the best judgment, should be the requirements in the selection of Senators. What has been collected here furnishes abundant proof that in Mr. Gowan's appointment these requirements were fulfilled, and, moreover, that it was a popular appointment, and, as was said in a leading journal, one opposed to the Government that appointed Mr. Gowan : 'Had the office been elective, the leading men of both, political parties would have united in choosing him. He never took an active part in politics. His appointment was not the reward of partizanship." *

He himself said, as has already been recorded :† "The

---

* "The Week," "Law Journal," etc.

† *Vide* reply to Address of County Council.

offer was entirely spontaneous. Why offered to me I can only surmise. I had neither suffered nor bled in political warfare, had not even drawn the political sword. * * I had no claim of this kind to bring me into notice. * * So I must surmise it was some supposed aptitude for the position that influenced my selection. You are good enough to think the intention of the founders of the Senate is fully carried out in my appointment."

" By his long services in the judiciary," said the able writer in " The Week," "and by his liberal and comprehensive views of law, as well as by his character and position, he is well fitted to represent his profession in the Senate, and to play a useful part in moulding legislation."

"With no political influence to wield," said the "Canada Law Journal," "with no political ambition to gratify, with no selfish purposes to serve, with means sufficient to make him thoroughly independent of any temptation to office, he is just the sort of man one likes to see in the halls of the Legislature. His recommendation for the position was the record of a long and useful public life, with abilities and experience far above the average. He will bring to the discharge of his legislative duties a calm, highly-trained judicial intellect, a mind well stored, not only with legal lore, but with a large fund of general information, which cannot but make him a most useful member of the Upper House."

Unexpectedly and unsought, the position came to him, and it is believed that there is not one member of the Senate more thoroughly independent or less trammelled by party than he is. An incidental observation by Mr.

Gowan, in his speech on the Franchise Bill, gives some indication of his views on this point. He remarked: "Men summoned to the Senate are reasonably taken from amongst those whose views are in the main in accord with the Government of the day, and because of some fitness for the position. Will the most rabid politician contend for a moment, that any one appointed to this honorable body, in accepting the summons, forfeits the right to think for himself in any measure that may come up, or surrenders his conscience to the sway of party, however much he may differ from his party on the particular case—of course not ; the Senate could in such case have no attractions for an honest man."

These are not the sentiments of one bound hand and foot by party, but of a man prepared to take a dispassionate view of all questions before the country.

A noteworthy incident must be mentioned in connection with a visit by Senator Gowan to Ireland, in the autumn of 1889.

The success of Irishmen abroad is always a pleasant theme with their countrymen at home. The career of Irishmen in Canada had attracted attention, and that of Senator Gowan especially was favorably referred to by the metropolitan press of Ireland.*

* The following article from a leading Dublin paper, of 22nd October, 1889, bears out the writer's observation in the text :—"We have often had occasion to refer with just pride in these columns to the notable successes of Irishmen abroad, which in no quarter of the world have been more frequent or conspicuous than in the Dominion of Canada. If proofs were required of the intellectual triumphs that our countrymen have achieved in the great dependencies of the British Empire named, they will be found in the able

During a brief stay in Dublin the Honorable Society of King's Inns conferred upon him the distinguished honor of a call to the Bar of Ireland.

The ruling body of this ancient society includes in its working members the Judges of the High Courts, as well as the leading Queen's Counsel and members of the Bar ; and we believe Senator Gowan's was the first case in which the resident of a colony, receiving his legal training wholly there, and away from his native country for over fifty years, was thus honored by an *unique* "act of grace," but, to use the words of a former Governor-General of

---

work of a distinguished Irishman, Mr. Nicholas Flood Davin, who has written the biographical history of the vast trans-oceanic community from the first days of its settlement. The slightest glance at its pages proves that the genius of Irishmen has contributed vastly to the growth of the western community, which has before it a future of such brilliant promise. Founded upon the best models of the motherland, traditions legal and social have been preserved, though not slavishly. They have been adapted to the wants and requirements of a new country which is leading in the van of civilization, and is in a position to teach its neighbors in jurisprudential capacity. Canada owes a vast deal to what is acknowledged as the imported intellect of men of Irish birth. By merit alone their advancement has been secured, and the colonial as well as the home community acknowledges that the tribute to genius is an universal one. It would be unnecessary to repeat the names of those statesmen who have helped to make modern history in Canada, but if they were to be set out at length it would be found that Irish names predominated amongst them. That of Lord Dufferin, sometime Governor-General of the Dominion, will first occur to popular recollection ; but working in coöperation with him, and thoroughly sympathizing with his enlightened aims and purposes, there have been a band of eminent Irishmen, whose records should not be forgotten, especially in times like these, when the bond of union between England and her colonies, and chiefly those of the neighboring west, have been drawn so closely together. To emphasize this connection is alike our policy and our interest. The establishment of the Imperial Colonial Institute, associated with the

Canada, speaking of the act, "In honoring him Ireland's Bar does honor to itself." There could have been no more worthy recipient, and it must have been as gratifying to the worthy Senator as it was to his friends in Canada and elsewhere. It was certainly also a high compliment to the Canadian Bar, of which he was one of the oldest members.

The "Irish Times" of the 6th November thus speaks of the graceful act: "Yesterday, at the sitting of the Court of Chancery, an unusual and interesting ceremony took place in the special honorary call to the Bar, by the

happy year of Her Majesty's Jubilee, is but the rational outcome of a common public opinion which England and her colonies alike share. Its objects contemplate not only a political, but a social purpose. Society in these countries desires to know more of the personality of the heads of the governments to whom authority is entrusted abroad, and wishes to take every opportunity of making acquaintance with them.

"For some time past a very interesting representative personage, who has borne much of the heat and burden of the day in setting up judicial and local governmental institutions in the great Dominion of Canada, has been sojourning amongst us. The name of the Honorable Judge Gowan is not by any means unknown in Ireland. An Irishman by birth, he went to Canada at a comparatively early age, and, by the exercise of exceptional talents, very soon attained the highest position at the Canadian Bar. For nearly forty-one years he was actively engaged in the judicial office. He was the youngest man ever entrusted with Her Majesty's commission as a Judge. In the early days of the Canadian settlement it was well that the services of so distinctively able a jurist should have been available. We have before us the records of his long term of labor, and during its course he earned the respect, not only of the Canadian Bar and public, but of reflecting jurists at home, who recognized in his decisions the maintenance of the constitutional principles of law, applicable to the state of the country, and especially important as setting a series of judicial precedents, which have become part and parcel of the common law of Her Majesty's western territorial possessions. A work, well known in

Lord Chancellor, of a distinguished Irishman, who has been staying for an interval amongst us, from the Canadian Dominion. The Benchers will be commended by every member of the profession, and the public will cordially endorse their action, for conferring such an honor upon the Honorable Senator Gowan. As we have said, Judge Gowan is a native of Ireland, and ranks high amongst the numerous body of able men who have risen to eminence in the colonies. * * We have no doubt that Senator Gowan very highly appreciates the honor done to him in associating him in fellowship with the Bar

---

Canada, written by Dr. John George Bourinot, Clerk of the House of Commons of Canada, bears ample testimony to the supreme influence that Judge Gowan exercised in modelling the municipal system of Canada. Naturally his long tried experience was appealed to, and it was owing to his enlightened and prudent counsels that so much was so rapidly done to place them upon a practical working basis. Our Canadian countrymen have elected Judge Gowan to the highest position which it is in their power to confer. Some years since he retired from the Bench, but he was immediately appointed to the Senate, a body corresponding to the House of Lords in England. Demands have since been made upon his learned judicial discretion, and never have been disappointed. No citizen of the Dominion occupies, at this time, a higher or better deserved position than Judge Gowan, Senator of Canada. In the highest ranks of English and Irish society he is honored, and it would be unfortunate if his countrymen were not to recognize his presence amongst them with a word of cordial and kindly acknowledgment. Men like Judge Gowan sustain the honor of Irish intellect abroad, and we cannot but feel pride in the successes of such lives of labor and of notable talent. Judge Gowan has not obtruded himself upon public notice, but we cannot allow a distinguished countryman to leave us without, for our part at least, bearing testimony to his most interesting and honorable career. A timely opportunity may yet be found to pay such a compliment to him as would be grateful to the sentiment alike of the people of Ireland, and of the loyal and noble Colonial community to which he belongs."

of his native country, and he will return to his high duties in Canada with, we should hope, a pleasing recollection of the hospitality shown to him, and the gratified consciousness that his abilities and character are known and appreciated alike by the legal profession in Ireland and by his countrymen generally."

The "Canadian Gazette" of the 14th November (published in London),* also refers to the call: "The legal community of Canada has been singularly honored by the distinction which the Irish Lord Chancellor has just conferred upon one of its representatives. On Tuesday of last week, at the sitting of the Court of Chancery in Dublin, Lord Ashbourne called to the Bar of Ireland the Honorable Judge Gowan, Senator of Canada, who for some time past has been sojourning in Ireland. Addressing Mr. Gowan, the Lord Chancellor said that, in view of his past distinguished career, he had great pleasure in

---

* The same issue of this journal also refers to Senator Gowan's career in Canada as follows: "The Honorable James Robert Gowan, L.L.D., upon whom this almost unique honor has been bestowed, can look back upon a long and honored career in Canada. By birth Judge Gowan is an Irishman, owning Wexford as his native county. Early in life he came with his father, the late Mr. H. H. Gowan, to Ontario, and in 1834, when only nineteen years of age, was admitted as a student by the Law Society of Upper Canada. In the succeeding years Canada was seething with unhappy rebellion, and in 1837-8, Lieutenant Gowan served his country in the 4th regiment of the North York Militia. His studies, however, still progressed, and in 1839 he was called to the Bar of Upper Canada, and four years later was appointed Judge of the district of Simcoe by the Baldwin-Lafontaine Reform Government, a position he filled with dignity and ability until his retirement in October, 1883. While on the Bench, Judge Gowan was able to render marked service in connection with legislative matters. Much of the reform and regulation of the

calling him to the Irish Bar as a member of a profession, in this his native country, which he ornamented in that of his adoption. The compliment was enhanced by the circumstance that the 'call' was a special one. Incidents of the kind were rare in the history of the Irish Bar, but in Canada, as in Ireland, the event would be recognized as a tribute of respect to the legal learning of the Dominion, which thus, in the person of one of its most prominent and respected representatives, was peculiarly acknowledged."

Canadian journals also made pleasant reference to the incident, appearing fully to "recognize it as a marked compliment to the whole legal profession in the country that one of their number should have been chosen for one of the most distinguished and seldom bestowed honors by the legal confraternity in Ireland."

Senator Gowan was only three years and six months at the Bar when he was appointed a Judge, and consequently was not entitled to be made a Queen's Counsel.

---

legal procedure of the several Courts in Ontario is due to his zeal and knowledge, while he gave invaluable aid in the codification of the Criminal and Statute law in the several confederated Provinces, and in the Dominion into which they formed themselves. He also served as chairman of the Board of Judges for Ontario from 1869 to 1887 ; as one of the commissioners appointed to enquire into the fusion of law and equity in Ontario, and as a member of the Royal commission to investigate the charges against the Ministry in connection with the historic 'Pacific Scandal.' In 1882, he was appointed to the High Court of Justice, and three years later was called to the Senate, where his name has recently been prominently associated with the framing and introduction of the present procedure of the Upper House with respect to applications for divorce. He has, in truth, been well described as a 'pioneer Judge, an erudite lawyer, and a leading mind in the great measures of law reform.' "

But after his retirement from the Bench, it is known, the dignity was offered to him. A new commission appointing a number of Queen's Counsels was issued during his absence in Europe, and his name appeared at the head of the list.

A brief word must be said of Mr. Gowan as a member of the Upper House, the Senate of Canada. With nearly half a century of constant and arduous work behind him, and the weight of three score years and ten upon him, when he entered Parliament as a Senator, the laborious habits of a life could not be shaken off, and the Senator's active mind impelled him to fresh exertion in a new sphere of usefulness.

It is not proposed to do more than note from the Journals and Hansard of the Senate, some particulars, to show how actively he has employed himself in Parliament.

In his first session, that of 1885, we find he was appointed to and served upon three joint committees of both Houses —on the Consolidation of the Statutes, on the Library, and on Printing; also on the committee on Standing Orders and Private Bills, and on several special committees, acting as chairman in three out of the six divorce cases that came before Parliament in the session of that year.

He introduced four bills into the Senate, three of them for amending the Criminal law. Of these four bills three passed the Senate, the fourth was rejected by a majority of one, but received the support of the Minister of Justice and the leader of the Opposition.

We observe, also, Mr. Gowan's name frequently appearing in the debates, speaking not merely on the bills he introduced, but on the N.-W. Property Bill, the Franchise Bill, the Maritime Court Bill, the Criminal Evidence Bill, the Temperance Act Amendment, on questions of Order, Divorce practice, Divorce cases and other matters. Indeed, his usefulness was admitted on all hands, and drew out even from the Opposition expressions of approval of his appointment.*

The session of 1886 again found the Honorable Senator in his place at Ottawa, a regular attendant at the House, actively engaged in the business going on and taking part in several debates, and the same was the case in the sessions of 1887, 1888 and 1889.†

---

* Senator Power, an eminent lawyer from Halifax, and a member of the Opposition, speaking on a bill introduced by Mr. Gowan, said: "I think that this bill, and two others which we have had before us already, go to show the wisdom exhibited by the Government in placing the honorable member from Barrie in this Chamber. From his position, my honorable friend learns what the defects are which the Judges who are now on the Bench, find in the Criminal law, and he is able, from his own experience, to recognize defects that have existed for some time. Legislation such as he has introduced, is just the kind of work which is calculated to give this Senate weight and respectability through the country; and I think that measures of this sort do us a great deal more service in public estimation than debates, extending no matter how many weeks, on the general question of our utility."

† An examination of the Journals and Hansard of the Senate shows that he was no idle member. During these four years he served every session on three important committees: "The Joint Committee on the Library of Parliament," "The Joint Committee of both Houses on Printing," and "The Committee on Standing Orders and Private Bills"—being chairman of the last mentioned committee in 1888. He also served as chairman on four committees upon as many contested Bills of Divorce. And he was a member, and acted upon the important special committee on "The Great Mackenzie Basin." He took part, also, in several debates in these sessions, speaking at considerable length on important questions touching legal matters.

In the session of 1888, he succeeded in carrying a very important scheme of reform, which deserves more particular notice. Early in that session, in an exhaustive and judicious speech, he drew attention to the subject of Marriage and Divorce in Canada and the United States, " showing emphatically that the fact that each State of the American Federation has sole jurisdiction over the subject, and has given the courts full power to grant divorces, has tended to the loosening of the marriage tie, and has been most injurious in that way to the morals and the sanctity of home life, on which depend so much of the happiness of peoples."*

Under the power given by the B. N. A. Act, as observed by Mr. Gemmill, the author of "Parliamentary Divorce," the Parliament of Canada has exercised itself since Confederation in passing numerous Acts for the dissolution of marriage ; but the system of procedure concerning Divorce Bills was incongruous, tedious and unsatisfactory, and a subject of constant reproach. The investigation of a case was divided between the House and a committee, which was almost always selected by the promoter of the bill, and the hearing of the evidence was conducted without regard to any settled rules of evidence. The rules of procedure were embarrassing to the practitioner, to officers, and to all engaged in administration. Moreover, they did not effectually guard against imposition on the House, and doubts and difficulties were constantly cropping up. The radical defect in the mode of

* From note by Dr. Bourinot, Clerk of the House of Commons.

appointing the committee to enquire into the facts was severely commented upon, and numerous complaints found expression within, as well as outside, the Senate chamber. It became evident that a reform was necessary. The work of reform was undertaken by Senator Gowan, and earnestly pressed on the consideration of the Senate. His scheme was entertained, and the subject referred to a special committee, embracing men of large parliamentary experience and the best legal ability in the House.

The subject was fully and carefully discussed in all its details by the special committee, and afterwards by a committee of the whole House. The body of rules submitted by Senator Gowan was finally, with some alterations, adopted by the Senate, on the 11th of April, 1888: the old rules being rescinded. These rules and orders placed procedure for divorce on as sound and satisfactory a footing as was possible without special legislation of a radical character.

This brief account of the matter sufficiently shows the necessity for the reform carried out, and its beneficial results have been proved in the test of actual working.

Dr. Bourinot, from whom we have already quoted, referring to the fact that " it had been frequently urged the time had come for removing the trial of these cases from the Legislative tribunal to the Courts of Law," adds : " Perhaps there may have been some reason found for the argument in the relatively loose procedure which existed in the Senate previous to 1888 ; but it can now be urged that the improvements, which have taken place in that procedure under the energetic and learned supervision of

Senator Gowan, in a great measure removes the objections that have been advanced against continuing so important a subject under the jurisdiction of Parliament."

Early in the session of 1889, Senator Gowan "called the attention of the House to the supposed uses and to the actual working of the grand jury system, in connection with criminal procedure in the several Courts of Canada; also to the value and importance of the Ontario County Crown Attorney system in the same connection."

And he asked "if the Government had had under consideration the propriety of submitting a measure to Parliament for the abolition of grand juries, and substituting therefor some general system of public prosecutors, similar to that which exists in Scotland; or whether the Government had under consideration the desirability of extending the benefits of the County Crown Attorney system, in connection with criminal procedure, to all the Provinces in the Dominion."

In submitting the question he delivered a long and carefully considered speech,* covering the whole ground, which elicited a full reply from the Honorable Mr. (afterwards Sir John) Abbott, then leader of the Government in the Senate, indicating a general assent to Senator Gowan's views, if with an expression of doubt as to whether public opinion was ripe for the change. Mr. Abbott is thus reported in Hansard: "I am sure the House has listened

---

* To give even an epitome of what was said would be to extend this Biography beyond the writer's design. The speech occupied more than twelve pages in the Senate Hansard of 1889. It was copied at length in the newspapers, and much commented upon.

with great interest, and is under deep obligations to my honorable friend, for the study and research which he has devoted to the question of the value of the grand jury in the administration of justice. It is probable that this venerable system is, perhaps, getting too venerable for the present age. * * The progress of our free constitutional system, under which offences are tried by Judges entirely independent of outside influences, has rendered the protection which the grand jury was calculated to give the citizen, practically unnecessary. * * It is to be feared that at this moment public opinion has not reached a point where it will be safe or judicious to attempt to do away entirely with the grand jury system, and substitute for it any other, no matter how well conceived it may be. I can say, however, in answer to my honorable friend's question, that the attention of the Government has been attracted to this question for a long time past, and they have had it under very serious consideration. * * I hope before long, perhaps next session, that the Government may be able to present a measure, having the tendency which my honorable friend's address indicates that he desires, and which I think his address is well calculated to hasten."

The subject was debated at the time, other Senators speaking for and against.

Honorable Mr. Scott, the leader for the Opposition, though not favoring the move, recognized Senator Gowan's careful study of the subject. " I listened," said he, " with a great deal of interest to the observations which fell from the honorable gentleman who brought this enquiry under the notice of the Senate, and he, no doubt, has given it a very exhaustive study, and his experience, from the position he held before he came to this Chamber, gave him a very large opportunity of studying the question.   *   *   "

The Honorable Mr. Kaulbach said : " I will not occupy the time of the House in making any extensive remarks ; but I am sure we must all be thankful to my learned friend from Barrie, for having brought this matter before us in the elaborate way he has done.   He has shown us that there is great laxity in the prosecutions for the Crown before grand juries, and miscarriage of justice in consequence."

The subject came up in a subsequent session, and was referred to by Sir John Thompson, in moving the second reading of his criminal code in the session of 1892.

The subjoined extract from his speech will show how entirely the Premier and Minister of Justice is in accord with Senator Gowan's views, as expressed in the latter's speech on the subject in 1889 :—

" The attention of the public has been directed very considerably to one change, which was mooted in connection with the reorganization of the law relating to criminal matters and criminal procedure, and that is the proposed abolition of the system of indictment by grand jury.   The attention of the Parliament and the public has been directed to that question very forcibly, indeed, by a member of the other branch of Parliament, a member to whom, I am sure, both Houses owe a great deal of gratitude for the pains and the care and the attention he has devoted to legislation during the many years of a useful and honorable life. I refer to Senator Gowan. He moved in the matter a year or two ago, and it was thought best that the attention of the public should be drawn even more strongly to the question than it was by the remarks he made on the subject in the Senate. The result was, as the House may remember, that a circular was sent to all the Judges in the country who have permanent criminal jurisdiction, and, indeed, all the officers charged with criminal prosecutions, calling their attention to the change which that learned gentleman thought desirable, and asking their opinions as to its propriety and expediency. It was felt that the opinions of those who are connected with the administration of criminal justice and have its care from time to time would be of great assistance to Parliament in framing any change that might be thought desirable; and we have had in response to that a great number of replies, most of which have been published, and some of which have come to hand since the publication of the returns by order of Parliament. The opinions upon that subject by those who were thus addressed were very divided indeed. Most of the Judges who are accustomed to administer justice without juries, in ordinary proceedings, were in favor of the change; the others were divided upon the subject; and it is impossible to deny, in view of so strong a division of opinion on the subject, that it seems unwise, in connection with this measure, to force that provision on the attention of Parliament at present. I must say that I concur personally in the opinion expressed in another place by the learned gentleman to whom I have made reference, and I think that in many respects the administration of justice would be improved, if we dispensed with the intervention of grand juries.

"I will say one word as to the disputed question of jurisdiction in this matter. The proposition has been mooted long ago, that this matter may be beyond the control of this Parliament, and may be more properly exercised by the Provincial Legislators. When we come to deal practically with the matter, that difference seems to me to vanish. It is not a question, after all, of whether the grand jury forms a part of the organization of the Courts or not, and, therefore, is under provincial control. It is a question whether, in criminal procedure, it is desirable to continue the exercise of functions by the grand jury. And in adopting an amended Criminal procedure, I take to be beyond a doubt that the question as to whether we should, or not, dispense with the services of the grand juries, is one which is included in that division of the Criminal law."

The Senator did not attend the Parliamentary session of 1890, having spent the winter of 1889-90 in Egypt and Palestine. But in the sessions of 1891-92 he was again in his place and taking an active share in the work of the Senate. But that to which he attended with untiring devotion was the work incumbent upon him as Chairman of the Select Committee on Divorce—a most important Tribunal of Parliament, for under the Legislative System of Parliamentary Divorce in Canada, all bills for divorce originate in the Senate, and under the rules of procedure Senator Gowan had introduced, all bills of divorce are referred to this select committee for investigation and report. The duties of this committee are similar to those performed by the Court of Divorce in England in respect to due notice to parties affected, the investigation of the allegations upon which the relief is sought, and what relief is to be granted, involving often difficult and delicate enquiries as to law and fact. The cases are conducted before the Select Committee by counsel, and with the formalities observed in a Court of Justice. The parties and their witnesses appearing and being examined *viva voce* before this Tribunal. Their report, though not conclusive, is almost without exception accepted by the Senate and the House of Commons to found the Act of Parliament upon it. Upon this committee the Senator must have found himself at home, and for four sessions he has acted as Chairman of this Select Committee of Divorce.*

Senator Gowan entertained strong objections to the establishment of a Court of Divorce for the Dominion, as did the late Sir John Macdonald, and to divorce for any cause save the matrimonial offence.†

---

* Mr. Gemmill, in his admirable work on Parliamentary Divorce, published in 1889, thus refers to Senator Gowan in the preface: "The author cannot properly close these remarks without expressing his deep sense of obligation to the Honorable James R. Gowan, L.L.D., who kindly perused the proof sheets during the progress of the work through the press, and aided him with many valuable suggestions. Those who are aware of the Honorable Senator's earnest and successful endeavors in the session of 1888—backed by all the knowledge acquired by him during his forty years' judicial experience—to place the practice of Parliamentary Divorce on a more certain and satisfactory footing than it had hitherto been, will well understand the writer's advantage in having the benefit of his mature judgment and advice."

† Senator Gowan's argument in favor of legislative divorce will be found in the Senate debates, but one or two extracts from his speech may be given :

Yet he maintained the doctrine of the Parliament of
Canada having full and paramount power to deal with

"The proceedings by private bill for divorce, designed, like other bills, to
attain its completion in an Act of Parliament, to a certain extent bear some
analogy to a suit in a Court of Justice; but it is not merely a proceeding between
party and party, though the primary immediate operation of the particular law
will be upon them. It is not a mere civil proceeding: the Act dissolves the
marriage of the parties, it also punishes the matrimonial crime committed by
one of them. It may, in a sense, be said to be a proceeding in *rem*, the *res*
being the marriage. Indeed, I would say it is neither contractual nor purely
penal, the operation being in respect to the marriage *status* of the parties, a
divine ordinance, as well as a domestic regulation, which the law has sanctioned, and has the power to regulate and control under the Constitution. In
entertaining application for divorce, and making a law to set the parties free
to marry again—changing their *status*—Parliament can properly bring in view
considerations of expediency, or public advantage. A Court of Justice is
necessarily restrained within fixed limits, and its procedure controlled by fixed
rules in matters assigned to it for adjudication between party and party.

"Parliament would be making a law, and the Supreme power of the State
(within constitutional limits of course), it would have to consider what would
most tend to the public good. The Courts but expound and administer law
which Parliament enacts. * *

"'Tis true, applications for divorce have always been based upon a specific
charge, and the facts necessary to support that charge established by satisfactory evidence, and, so far, the proceeding is *quasi judicial.* Inquisition is
made, and the truth or falsity of the facts alleged determined, and to that
extent there is an analogy to the proceedings of a Court. But whether, by
reason of the facts proved, the prayer of the petitioner should be granted, opens
considerations for Parliament which could not be permitted to Judges when
called upon to pronounce what the judgment should be.

"Further, in criminal cases the Executive may be called upon to decide
whether, in view of all the facts and circumstances, the judgment of the Court
should be carried into effect or modified.

"Now, Parliament may be said to unite in itself all these three duties and
functions. It decides whether the charges are proved, whether they constitute
such a case as should entitle the party to a special Act for relief, and what

cases before them without **being bound by the principles laid down by the House of Lords or by their decisions.**[*]

---

relief, if any, should be granted to the party, in view of all the circumstances : and Parliament may and ought always to have in regard, not merely the question as it affects the parties, but the effect in relation to morals and good order —the effect which the passing a particular law might have upon the well-being of the community. Parliament, as the supreme power, has its duties and responsibilities, and cannot compromise the well-being of society, which has been entrusted to it under the Constitution.

"These are the considerations which brought me to the conclusion that, in the present aspect of the question, any delegation of the power respecting divorce would be inexpedient.

"Parliament can deal with matters in the abstract ; judicial decisions are, by their very nature, concrete, and all the Judge professes to do is to decide the case before him on ascertained legal principles."

[*] In the Tudor-Hart Divorce Case, under an old Rule of the Senate regulating procedure, which said that in unprovided cases reference should be had to the decision of the House of Lords, it was urged that the Parliament, in granting or withholding relief upon Bills of Divorce, were bound by decisions and principles acted on in the House of Lords. The subjoined extracts from the debates on the case will show how entirely Senator Gowan repudiated that view : "This seems to me to be an entire misconception of the scope and object of Rule, which relates solely to practice and procedure, and is on its face merely directory. A Rule having the substantial effect contended for would be bad, and would be out of place in 'Rules of Proceeding.' Under the Constitutional Act of Canada, Parliament has no restrictions, and none can exist except imposed or enacted by Parliament itself. The Senate and the House of Commons can each regulate its own procedure, but neither body, nor both bodies together, could diminish or control the substantial action of Parliament, or the Constitution would be at an end. In shaping action or legislation on a Bill of Divorce upon facts in evidence before us, we naturally look to the House of Lords, hoping for light, and to see what others have done in cases similar to those in which we are called upon to deliberate and act. But we have never bound ourselves to accept their decisions as authoritative and conclusive. We follow 'precedents' where they commend themselves to our judgment, and we decline to follow them where they do not, and

And he succeeded in securing the affirmance by Parliament of an important principle : the equal responsibility of man and woman, and their equal right to

---

rightly so, for the decisions of the House of Lords on Bills of Divorce have not the weight that attaches to the decisions of the regular legal tribunals. The 'Precedents' in the House of Lords reach back for some two hundred years from 1858, when the Divorce Court was established. These precedents abound during times not conspicuous for purity in social life, or when legislation exhibits any marked effort for promotion of morality. The manners and customs, if not corruptions, of classes fashioned opinion, and the higher moral tone and the controlling power of the healthy public opinion of modern times was in those times little known. In legislative dissolution of marriages, the provisions of a Divorce Bill were, however, in the discretion of a majority, which could adopt them to particular cases and enact as to the majority seemed meet. I must say one does find old cases before the House of Lords where it is difficult to reconcile the decisions with Christian ethics, and occasionally some indications appear of notions and sentiments (due probably to a highly-artificial condition of society) not in unison with our simple common sense views of right and wrong. We never have accepted the 'precedents' of the House of Lords in matters of substance as our rule of right, nor are we bound to follow their action, or shape our decisions to square with theirs."

" * * We never, I repeat, accepted the principles and precedents of the House of Lords as our rule of right, and we have not followed them. Part of the Empire—in confederation under a common sovereign—yet with a Constitution similar in principle to that of the United Kingdom, we Canadians have the making, moulding and developing of the laws. The recognition or rejection of principles which shall prevail in our community, and to us it belongs exclusively to enact and declare as a Parliament in all that concerns the welfare and good government of Canada, one iota of this power, I for one, am unwilling to surrender or abate. I would again emphatically reassert the position that we are not restrained in our action under the British North America Act, for we have not imposed any restrictions on the exercise of our power in making a law touching Divorce. We act according to our 'wisdom and discretion,' upon the facts and circumstances in each case, and in legislating consideration of what is just and what will best guard public morals and the interests of society, must ever be our guiding star."

divorce on proof of adultery, a principle not recognized in England.[*]

On several occasions he spoke at length on Divorce Bills. He took part also in several debates on various subjects in the sessions of 1891 and 1892 on matters of privilege— Criminal Law Bills, the Grand Jury System, the Administration of Justice in the North-West, the Canada Temperance Law, the Codification of the Criminal Law, the Temperance Act Amendment ; and so likewise in the session of 1893, on the Criminal Code Bill, on the Law of Evidence in Criminal Cases, on the Administration of Justice, on the Composition of the Select Committee on

---

[*] "With respect to Divorce in England, one is struck with the marked, and, I must think, unjust, discriminations made between the sexes in respect to matrimonial offences, and the prejudices which existed, and still exist, against equal right of relief to the woman as well as the man. They have been much modified in recent times, it is true, but they yet remain and find expression in the Statutes. I am not aware of such prejudices ever existing in Canada, not in Ontario at all events, and I can find no indications of such in the several Divorce Acts of the Parliament of Canada, but the reverse, as an examination of our precedents and the grounds upon which Divorce Acts were passed, as set forth in the preambles, will clearly show, the subject of divorce passed to the Parliament of Canada, in the distribution of legislative powers under the Constitution, absolutely and at large."

After reviewing the House of Lords cases on Divorce down to 1857, when the Divorce Act was passed, and showing the gradual progress in England of a better and purer feeling in Parliament and amongst public men, and the efforts to secure equal right to the wife in 1857, Senator Gowan proceeded : " But prejudices prevailed, and the partial and unjust provisions towards the wife were retained. Thus, up to the last moment the legislative power of the Lords could be exercised in granting Divorce in England, we see a narrow and unjust sentiment prevailed on this subject. Outside of mere procedure, could we look for pure light in the ' precedents ' they established, much less broadly accept them as our rule of right ? * * Indeed, only in four cases before

Divorce and Appointment of Professional Men, on certain constitutional objections to a bill for appointment of a Deputy Speaker to the Senate, and on Prohibition, besides dealing with all cases before the Select Committee on Divorce, in which, as Chairman, he presented the reports. Two of these subjects may be further referred to. In the bill for the Amendment of the Law of Evidence in Criminal cases, it proposed to allow the evidence of the parties accused of crime. Senator Gowan had previously on more than one occasion voted against a similar measure, but he did not hesitate to support this bill, giving his reasons for a change of mind.

---

the case of 1886, have Divorce Acts been passed on application by women. The feeling was against them, and reform moves slowly where manners and class influences largely mould lines of thought. As a Canadian, I rejoice that a different and a better sentiment prevailed here. The Parliament of Canada, since Confederation (1867), has passed thirty Divorce Acts; eleven are in favor of women whose husbands were proved to be guilty of adultery, and of the eleven some seven were cases in which Acts for the dissolution of marriage could not have been obtained if the principles and precedents acted on in the House of Lords had been entertained and acted upon by the Parliament of Canada. We never, I repeat, accepted them as our rule of right, and we have not followed them. * * Precedents in the House of Lords before the formation of a Divorce Court, 1857, go to establish these propositions: First. That a husband aggrieved only by adultery might obtain a Divorce almost as a matter of right. Second. That a wife had no title when she is aggrieved only by adultery. Third. But that the provisions of a Divorce Bill being in the discretion of Parliament, that Parliament might mould and adapt its relief according to the exigency of the case, and take care that justice was done, its power being supreme. If there be no precedent to fit the case now before us and be followed, the facts in evidence justify us making one in granting the relief asked, and every principle of morality and justice appeals to us to declare that relief should be granted to a woman under circumstances such as these. The preamble of the bill in this case, reciting the petition, sets forth

The other subject was a Government bill introduced by a Minister for the appointment of a Deputy Speaker to the Senate. This measure he strongly opposed, speaking at great length in support of his view that the bill was objectionable, an invasion of the prerogative and unconstitutional, being beyond the power conferred on the Parliament of Canada by the British North America Act. The bill was carried by the Government in the Senate by a majority of members, but when it went to the Commons it was there opposed on the same ground, and had ultimately to be withdrawn by the Government.*

More could be said about Senator Gowan's work in Parliament, but enough has been brought out to show that from the time he entered the Senate, notwithstanding his advanced age, he has been a persistent and useful worker.

the facts and the prayer for the dissolution of the marriage of the petitioner and respondent. The Committee find she has proved the allegations of her petition, and established the adultery charged." * *

The bill for the relief of the wife passed in the Tudor-Hart case, and thus Parliament affirmed the principle contended for : " If there is one broad and palpable result of Christianity which we ought to regard as precious, it is that it has placed the seal of God Almighty upon the equality of man and woman with respect to everything that relates to these rights ; and the opposite would lead to the degradation of woman."

* We give some extracts from Mr. Gowan's speech as reported in Hansard :
" * * The question is a difficult one, involving matter of construction and constitutional capacity, and demands a fuller investigation than could well be given in a large deliberative body. It is a matter upon which experts are not agreed, and the facts bespeak additional caution. As I said, I shall only be able to indicate some salient points that occur to me, but though they may not be presented in the most orderly manner or argued out properly, my honorable friend and legal leader will not pass them by, for his character as an honorable, courteous gentleman and accomplished lawyer has preceded him

Imperial distinction, a mark of honor directly emanating from Her Most Gracious Majesty the Queen, every British subject both in the Colonies and elsewhere, of course highly values, but until of late years it was rarely given for good service in the Colonies, unconnected with Imperial rule. It was bestowed for distinguished service in the Army and Navy or in the Diplomatic Corps, or for some special service touching Imperial interests. No doubt, the Empire in its creation and extension was the work of the Army, the Navy and Diplomatists. But the Empire has been created, and its consolidation and perpetuation belongs to the Civil servants and to Statesmen, and the fact has been recognized that men who have done service to the State in Colonial fields, and are found deserving should receive Imperial recognition. Senator Gowan had no political

to this House, and his manner of life for at least seven years in a calm atmosphere will have shown him the duty and the importance of weighing all that can be said, where there is a conflict of opinion. It is a serious matter to meddle with the British North America Act except upon cogent grounds, and never should it be attempted, unless the authority to do so is clear. Some alterations in the British North America Act were made and sanctioned by the Imperial Parliament; a doubtful exercise of power by the Parliament of Canada, was healed or confirmed; but never, so far as I am aware, has the substance of the machinery for legislation been touched. I look with apprehension on any attempt to do so. I am free to admit the bill aims at remedying a practical inconvenience that has occurred in the past, but very serious difficulties were at these times obviated within the lines of the Constitution. Here there is no pressing urgency, and certainly none for action, as some contend, by arrogating powers not ours. The session is almost at a close, and if any emergency arose, such as occurred in Mr. Speaker Macpherson's time, it might be met in the way then adopted. So far as I am informed, all precedent is against it, as honorable gentlemen will see by examining the records. * * The first consideration that presents itself to

record to attract attention, but his long and varied services might well claim for him Imperial recognition. It was known the late Sir John Macdonald desired it for him, and that Sir John Abbott and Sir John Thompson thought him worthy of such recognition, as did also men of high standing in England, who knew something of his career in Canada. It accordingly came when Honors were conferred by the Queen in May, 1893. A companionship in the most distinguished order of Saint Michael and Saint George was conferred upon him " in recognition of his long and valuable services to the State," and we venture to think no more deserving object of her Gracious Majesty's recognition in this way could be found in the Province in which he has lived and labored so long.

When the honor conferred by the Queen was made

---

my mind is the fact that ours is a written Constitution, the Government of Canada being one of enumerated powers, the British North America Act being the instrument that specifies them, and wherein authority should be found for the exercise of any legislation it assumes the power to pass. The whole frame-work of our Constitutional Act is the creature of an Imperial Statute. While the power of the Imperial Parliament is practically unlimited and absolute even to changing the Constitution, our power is limited and restrained by the instrument—our written Constitution, and especially it seems to me in all that pertains to any integral part of machinery devised for legislation, where power is not plainly conferred, the exercise of it is impliedly prohibited, I must think, for the intent of the grant would otherwise be defeated by such exercise. What the true intent and meaning of the British North America Act is, so far as it touches this bill, it will be proper to consider, in the light of recognized rules of construction. I take it the prime object should be to ascertain the meaning of the Legislature, and the rule seems to be applicable with special force to a written Constitution, not to attempt to interpret that which needs no interpretation, but to take the whole Statute together to arrive at the legislative intent. The preamble to the British

public, the press of the country with one voice expressed warm approval.

. The foregoing sketch presents but a brief and imperfect outline of the life of a distinguished patriot.

Looking back on his varied and abundant engagements one is brought to the conclusion that he had a passion for work, which he freely indulged, and that his ever present desire was to be unostentatiously useful in his adopted country. General and spontaneous recognition of honorable and useful public services rarely comes to any man before his career has finally closed, but Senator Gowan, with, it is hoped, a further period of usefulness before him, has secured the appreciation of numerous friends, and pronounced recognition of his public services, as this brief

---

North America Act recites that it is 'expedient not only that the Constitution of the legislative authority in the Dominion be provided for, but also that the nature of the Executive Government therein be declared.' * * And further, let it be borne in mind the proposed bill touches the prerogative and appointing power in enabling the Speaker of the Senate to appoint a presiding officer for the Senate, with the powers, privileges and duties of a Speaker—and the bill proposes to validate his every act. Now, every one knows the prerogative is not to be prejudiced or taken away without clear enactment, involving the assent of Her Gracious Majesty, and the rule of construction is in accordance with our highest and best sentiments. The prerogative is part of the band that unites us with tender clasp to the dear old land—that unites us Britons beyond the Sea, to the greatest Empire the world has ever known. I ask where is the power to be found in our Constitutional Act to alter an integral part of the Constitution—the Senate— in the machinery for legislation? Is it to be found in section 18, as alleged? I think not. The context and the subject-matter in view forbid it. The power is given to each House respectively to secure freedom of speech, to prevent disorder, to punish inside and outside offenders for contempts in

sketch has shown—from the people and the people's representatives amongst whom he lived and worked for half a
century ; from the Bar of the Courts over which he presided ; on repeated occasions, from the Government of the
country and its Ministers, as well as the Queen's representatives in this Dominion, and even the Queen herself has
been pleased to confer an honorable distinction upon him
"in recognition of his long and valuable services to the State."

To those who seek for the moving causes of his success,
it may be said that he was by nature peculiarly well endowed, inheriting a father's indomitable will and a mother's
refined intellectuality. Always actuated by an earnest
purpose, whatever he undertook he carried to a successful
issue ; having put his hand to the plough, he never looked
back. The thoroughness of his work was remarkable, and

---

certain cases, to make inquiries, and other kindred subjects that might be
mentioned, but it does not touch a matter of this kind. My honorable friend
seems to build on this frail foundation. For my part, in looking at it I could
scarcely think of any even plausible argument, anything that could be laid hold
of with sufficient firmness even for the purpose of discussion. Then comes the
point—and it seems to me the only point—under the 91st section, and I am
not surprised that my honorable friend should take the view he does ; it is the
only possible foundation which occurs to me for advocating the cause of legislating in the manner proposed by this bill. The suggestion is that under the
general terms there is general power to make laws for the peace, welfare, and
good government of Canada ; but I must say that I think, as at present advised, it is a very forced construction to regard it as supporting this proposed
measure. The bill relates to the construction of the Senate, and how it may
hereafter be composed. The Senate cannot act without a presiding officer,
and the bill relates to the composition of the Senate, how it shall be made
complete in case of the absence of the Speaker. Now, what does the 91st
section provide ? It deals altogether with matters foreign to the aim and
purpose of the bill before us. The clause 91 gives a detailed enumeration

his arguments were always exhaustive. Can we wonder at his success! Failure under such conditions would be incredible.

In his social and domestic relations the Senator was particularly happy. Of a thoughtful and kindly disposition, he took the greatest pleasure in forwarding the best interests of those about him, and, in the wider circle of his acquaintance, there is many a young man who bears him life-long gratitude for timely advice and material help. Open hearted and generous, no worthy charity has gone without his liberal aid, and no deserving individual ever appealed to him in vain ; and yet he was not a rich man— at least in his earlier years. He inherited no large fortune, nor did he speculate in any way with the moderate means at his command, thus avoiding the financial rocks which

showing what was in the mind of the Legislature in using the term ' peace, welfare, and good government of Canada,' and 'that is the point we are to arrive at—What was in the mind of the Legislature in passing this Act ? What in using the terms peace, welfare, and good government of Canada ? Not the machinery for legislation or any part of the Constitution itself. Had it been so intended, I take it that apt words would have been used, judging from other provisions of the British North America Act. * * This bill, if it becomes law, gives us a prolocutor appointed by the Speaker or by the Senate, with all the powers and privileges which the Queen's Commission confers on a Senator appointed in the manner prescribed by the Constitutional Act. An important duty and trust for a public purpose, I must believe, cannot be assigned to one whom the Crown has not constituted. Let me say a word further : The matter is of a nature that His Excellency the Governor-General may feel bound to consider it his duty to reserve, and it seems our duty to give all the aid possible in considering the point, and that we should have the amplest discussion to throw as much light on the subject as possible. Doubtless His Excellency would receive the opinions of the law officers of the Crown in Canada, that the several bills submitted

wreck so many; but, rather, by a judicious and careful management of his affairs, and by living scrupulously within his income, has he accumulated a comfortable fortune.

Possessed at all times of sufficient means, he was free from the many temptations which beset the improvident, and was ever able to give an undistracted mind to the duties of his high office, and his leisure time to congenial studies and, as we have seen, to important public labors.

In personal appearance, Judge Gowan, in 1843—his contemporaries tell us—was a handsome young man, of tall and commanding figure, with an intellectual forehead, a firm mouth, and a clear, keen eye. His very presence compelled respect and admiration. He formed a unique figure on the Bench—an ideal Judge.

In 1893, after half a century of unremitting public labors, in the seventy-ninth year of his age, the venerable Senator stands before us,* his hair tinged with gray, but with the

---

are right and constitutional; but, if I am not mistaken, His Excellency would not be bound by that, and he might reserve this bill, and he might send it over for the opinion of his Government, and they doubtless would take the opinion of the law officers on the subject; and, therefore, I say it is very proper that the fullest inquiry should be made. I am sure there can be no desire on the part of any one to arrive at any other conclusion than that which is right in this matter. In any case it would certainly not be pleasant if any Act passed here was sent back disallowed; it would be an unpleasant thing, and I certainly would not like it. Now, while I agree that some provision might be desirable to obviate the inconvenience, if it arises, of a temporary vacancy in the Chair—I think it ought to be done and would like to see it done in a constitutional way, and I think that the method by passing this bill would not be a constitutional one.

* The Senator's portrait on the first page is from a photograph taken in 1891.

same clear, fearless eye, softened somewhat with the kind-
liness of age, vigorous in mind, rich in years and honors—
honors bestowed upon him by a grateful country and an
appreciative sovereign. He forms one of the few links
still binding us to a generation fast passing away—men
who laid the foundations of this free country broad and
deep, to whom we younger ones of the present day owe a
debt of gratitude which can never be repaid.

Any general estimate of character of a man still living
could not well be expected, but those who have known
Senator Gowan best and longest think most highly of him,
and it may be truly said that he is everywhere "under the
tongue of good report,"* and has never lost a personal
friend.

For more than fifty years the Senator's home has been
in Barrie; his residence, with its ample grounds, is beauti-.
fully situated on Kempenfeldt Bay, an arm of Lake Simcoe; he has also a charming summer residence in the
picturesque lake district of Muskoka, "Eileangowan," a
wooded island of over four hundred acres, about forty
miles north of Barrie.

---

* An accident befel the Senator, at Ottawa, about a year ago, which was
at first supposed to be serious, drew out a general expression of sympathy.
An extract from an article which appeared in "The Ottawa Citizen" shows
the general tenor: "The venerable and estimable Senator is a man who, by
the eminent and distinguished character of his public services, no less than by
the excellence and usefulness of his private life, has established a claim upon
the public consideration which all classes will feel and be ready to recognize.
* * "

www.ingramcontent.com/pod-product-compliance
Lightning Source LLC
Chambersburg PA
CBHW020230030726
47497CB00009B/3022